Drop Dead

Drop Dead

K.B. Steinmetz

Library of Congress Control Number:		2011907791
ISBN:	Hardcover	978-1-4628-7275-6
	Softcover	978-1-4628-7274-9
	Ebook	978-1-4628-7276-3

To order additional copies of this book, contact:
Xlibris Corporation
1-888-795-4274
www.Xlibris.com
Orders@Xlibris.com
96158

REWIND

The door was open; we were on a major highway. I was in the back of the van with my hands tied.

I was drowsy from the night before but managed to stay awake. Lar Mandel #2 (but we just call him Lar M or M2) was up front, talking to two other guys.

Soon, one of them came over to me and pulled me up. He was big and ugly and had a bad odor, but that's not the point. (His name is now Big Ugly Guy.)

They were talking in a language that I couldn't understand (most likely Latin). Big Ugly Guy started to push me. He then untied my hands and shoved me over to M2.

All three stared at me. M2 soon grabbed my arm. He gave me an evil smile.

His tight grip numbed my arm. He dragged me over to the open door. His strong muscular arm tilted my head in an angle so I could get a good look at the pack of cars behind us.

Then he pulled me back in. He gave me an evil smile again. He was going to push me off the van.

M2 opened the van door more. Soon enough, he looked at me. He put his two hands on my shoulders.

Then without a doubt, he grabbed my neck and pulled me back. He was getting ready to shove me out of the vehicle.

Like any normal girl, I was not just going to stand there waiting to die. I grabbed his arm and flipped him. (Got that from boot camp.)

After he got up, I only realized that I should not have done that. A rush of steam ran through his veins. He stomped over to me.

He grabbed my arm but tightened the grip even more. I winced. I tried to get away, but it didn't help. Again, he pulled me back, and then out of nowhere he forced me forward.

I lost my balance and flew into the air . . .
Wait!

Forget this. It has nothing to do with what you need to know now!

CHAPTER 1

People nowadays often think that if a parent is a criminal or some outlaw, the teen is going to turn out no good.

My parents were worse than any criminal. My parents were part of the Mafia. (What do you think about that?) However, I am not that bad (yet).

This story begins in 2008. I was fourteen years old. Moreover, as any other kid, if your parents were *defined* as "outlaws," you would not be very popular. I walked through the halls at my school in silence, blocking out all of the gossip and hand motions being made toward me.

Finally, I reached my ninth-period class. I sat down and waited for the teacher to speak. I looked up at the blackboard to check for homework. Then my eyes focused on the teacher. Nevertheless, I got sidetracked by the boy standing beside her. I kept staring at him. I don't know why. I never got interested in boys (guys). They were stupid. However, I could definitely make an exception for this one.

The bell rang, and the teacher clapped her hands to get our attention. "Class, I would like you to meet Josh Brian. He is a new student," Mrs. McGee, our teacher, said. "You may go sit down across Natalie."

Without thinking, I took my pointer finger and poked my chest with disbelief. Josh was going to be sitting down across from me.

He made his was down the aisle and sat down in his designated seat. For the rest of the class, I would turn my head to look over at him every couple of minutes. (I couldn't help myself.) Every time I did that, I noticed that he would be looking at me.

After class, I stormed out of the classroom. While I was walking swiftly away, my books fell. I bent down to pick them up. When I got up, I heard, "Natalie!" I looked toward the person who called my name; it was Josh. "Wait up," he called.

I decided to wait for him. After all, I couldn't be mean to him; he was new. He made his way toward me. As soon as he was about three feet away from me, Cassandra had to come.

(Cassandra? Hum? The only way that I can describe Cassandra would be to say that she was a mean, idiotic female who likes to get what she wants.)

She walked up and stopped Josh from coming over to me. "Hey, what are you doing?" she asked.

"I'm going over to talk to Natalie," Josh said.

"Her? You don't want to talk to her. She's bad."

I looked over at her. Ever since sixth grade, she was trying to ruin my life. Thanks to her, I only have one friend, Carlos. She took a glance at me and smiled. I didn't do anything but walked away.

Josh looked at Cassandra. "Don't worry about it. No one likes her. You know why? It's because her parents are part of the Mafia," Cassandra explained. "And we all know that she's part of it, just that she won't admit it." Following that statement, Cassandra pulled Josh her way, and they walked down the hallway.

Josh's face lit up a bright red color, as if he knew something.

I walked home alone. No one to talk to and no one to laugh with, but I didn't mind it. Ever since my parents became partners in the Mafia, I was alone. (Meaning, like, forever.)

That night after supper, I was doing my homework. However, like any eighth grader, we always did our homework after supper so we got out of helping with the dishes.

Well, anyway, where was I? Oh yes, I was doing my homework when the phone rang. My dad *Jed Maclusta* got up from his newspaper and got it.

After he hung up, he told my mom Kristine that the head of the Mafia, Lar Mandal, was calling an emergency meeting.

I know it's confusing. I'll give you a bit of background. The Mafia is led by two twin brothers. Lar Mandel is the leader, and his brother, Lar Mandel #2 (most often referred to as M2), is in second command. But since my parents sort of became Lar Mandel's favorite, M2 has somehow been grumpy.

Then, like all parents, they asked me if I would be okay while they are gone. Doing a fourteen-year-old's gesture, I put my hands on my hips and said I was going to be *just fine.*

So they kissed my forehead and left. I watched them leave through the window. As soon as their car zoomed out of the driveway, I hopped onto the couch and turned on the television.

I guess you know what this means; that's the end of homework. I calculated the time they left—six thirty. Whenever they called an emergency meeting, it would always take about two hours.

Two hours went by in a flash. By eight thirty, I was actually tired. However, instead of going to bed, I decided to stay up until my parents came home.

I stayed up longer than I intended. With it now being nine thirty and with no sign of them, I started to get worried. Then I remembered what my dad said, "Never trust the Mafia; they are very sneaky and dangerous." (I then wondered why they ever joined in the first place.)

I stayed up the rest of the night. My parents were still not home. By morning, I was panicking, until the doorbell rang. I went to get it. When I opened the door, a man was there. He was about in his midthirties, with brown hair and hazel eyes. He had a little indented shape of a curve on his left cheek. Obviously from a fight. He stood there staring at me when he said, "Your parents are dead." His voice was deep, like the sound of death. He handed me a case, tilted his hat, and left.

I opened the case; there was a gun and a note:

Miss Natalie,

This is what is left of your parents. I hope that you understand that you have my deepest condolences. Your parents were great partners, but they made one big mistake. I am sorry things had to end up like this.

Head of the Mafia,
Lar Mandal

CHAPTER 2

Two Years later . . .

Since the night of my parents' death two years ago, I've been on the computer every night, looking for anything that could or would lead me to the proof that the Mafia killed my parents. Last night, I found out that they were in the area. Even though I was sixteen, I felt a little like Nancy Drew.

It was after school. I was at home when the door rang. I turned off my iBook and went to get the door. It was my friend Carlos. We were friends since we were little. Both of our parents were with the Mafia, and somehow we just have gotten to know each other, and now, we're friends. Well, more like best friends.

He had a frantic look on his face. You could see the sweat bursting through his tan skin. And no, he is not Puerto Rican.

He walked in as I shut the door. "What's with you?" I asked. I spoke with hesitation, still shocked about the news I recently found about the Mafia being in the area. There was one thing that I still couldn't understand. Thinking back to when the man gave me the gun case filled with money. Why did Lar Mandal say that my parents made one big mistake in the letter? Why did he write me a letter? The Mafia never wrote letters. Well, none that I saw in the movies, anyway.

It took him a while to catch his breath. That was when I noticed the bag he was carrying.

"They're after us," he huffed.

"Who's after us?"

"The Mafia. They somehow figured out that I was your friend, and they want some questions answered."

The Mafia must have known that I was on their case. That meant that I was getting close on their trail. (It only took me two years. Only later in time, I figured out that that's not the reason they wanted me.) I started to smile and jump up and down. Then I realized the way Carlos was staring at me, so I stopped and listened to what he had to say.

"You got to get packed, we have to go," Carlos stuttered.

"Why? Are they coming here?" I was confused; they didn't know where I lived. I moved last month. I walked over and sat down on the sofa.

"Well, are you going to move or not?" he asked.

I then looked up and realized that he was serious. Well, I knew that he was serious, I just didn't know that he meant *now*. I finally obeyed and walked into my room to get packed. It only took me five minutes to get everything together.

Then just like how they would. I took a map of the county and laid it on the table. I fixed the light so it beamed down on the table. In addition, just for an extra touch, I turned off all the lights. Well, all but the one over the table. It made me feel like a detective. "Okay, this is what we are going to do . . ."

It didn't take us long to get out of the neighborhood, for a multiple of reasons. To start, we're young, we have energy. In addition, the second reason was, well, one of the biggest illegal mobs (so to speak) was after us. I think that would help our brain realize that we wanted to go faster.

Then we were gone, sort of like ghosts. *He's there, and then he's gone.*

With that, we ran and ran. The problem with running away from the Mafia was that no matter how far you run, they always find ways to get you. Sort of like a Chuck Norris. *You can run, but you can't hide.*

The nice thing about where I lived is that out of town is, like, a *jungle.* I say this because there is nothing but trees, rivers, streams. *Wildness,* I guess you could call it.

Apparently, Carlos didn't like it. "Oh, come on, Natalie," Carlos complained.

I looked back at him. "You always say you want to be like Crocodile Dundee. Besides, this would be the best to practice. Just think of how Dundee would think of you," I convinced.

Man, you would like of him as a city kid. He hates the outdoors. Well, sort of anyway. He didn't bother me after that. Until that is, he fell into . . . what you wanna call it? A mud ditch? I think that is what you call it. Well, you know, a big hole with mud in it. Yeah, he just happened to be walking and slipped, and well, I think you can picture it yourself. (It was very dirty.)

"Did Dundee have to go through this?" Carlos asked with mud dripping down his face.

I did not know what to say. "Well, of course. He went through worse," I returned, not really knowing whether it was true or not. Honestly, I did not really know Crocodile Dundee, except that he's like kind of cool.

It was now 6:30 p.m. I hated that it was getting darker. I was on my laptop when a big red light flashing came upon it. It said, *You thought you could run?*

Carlos was over at the fire that he made. For a boy who was in Boy Scouts, he didn't learn that much. Even I could build a fire that was better than that, and I was not even in Girl Scouts.

I was the *watcher*, so to speak. It was windy. The normal reaction toward that would make me a little cold. All I could really do was go on the laptop and hunt for clues. I tried to concentrate, but it was hard. I kept on hearing noises. Finally, when my head was about to blow, I got up and went to find out what that noise was.

With nothing to defend myself, I went into the darkness. I know that it might make you think that might be odd. Well, to tell you the truth, when I was about thirteen, I was shot in the arm. It didn't feel very good, so I don't want anyone else to have to go through that. (Even if they are a criminal.)

I walked over to see if Carlos was asleep. Sadly, he was. Therefore, I just kept on walking. As I was walking through the dark, misty gloom of the place, I heard the noise again. That was when I realized that we weren't the only ones in this rough environment.

I thought back to when I was in the CIA (Central Intelligence Association) with my parents. Yeah, my parents were all over the place, my teacher would always tell me, "Never blow your cover. No matter what." I then crouched to the ground. I walked as quietly as I possibly could. No more than a second later, I heard a twig snap behind me. I spun around. There was that guy, the one who came to my house that one morning to inform me about my parents' death. Why was he here after two years?

He stood there like he did once before, not saying a word. Then as if he were doing a replay of the past, he knelt down and put a gun case on the ground. I looked at it, confused as could be. Then I looked up, hoping to be able to talk to him. Nevertheless, he was gone. Like a ghost, I talked to you about in the beginning of the chapter. *He was just here, but now, he's gone.*

I look around, hoping to find him. Finally, I spotted him, but he held a remote that could only mean one thing . . .

I had to think fast. I quickly dropped the gun case. Hoping to miss the explosion, I start to run. Unfortunately, I didn't run fast enough; the gun case exploded. I flew into the air. My ears popped. I was unconscious.

I woke to the sound of guns. My head hurt, and I didn't know where I was. I lifted my head to see my surroundings. It was pitch-black. The only thing I could make out was the smell. The smell was horrid, as if there were dead things in here.

I heard coughing. Someone else had to be in here with me (probably Carlos). I wanted to ask who it was, but my mouth would not make out the words. I was cold, hungry, and undetermined.

It felt as if hours went by. I tried to get up. My chest hurt uncontrollably. It was painful to breathe. I put my hand where it hurt and then tried once more to get off the cold wooden floor. I made it. I staggered to the door. I could make out the doorknob from the way it was shaped.

I slowly turned it with the hand that was free, scared of who might be outside waiting for me. I gingerly opened it. I first looked out to see who would be watching. Surprisingly, no one was there so I made my way out of the room. I soon lost my balance and started to fall. As I was going down, I felt a strong, muscular hand catch me. I wrapped my hands around the hand to catch my balance.

As soon as I stood up straight, the man was gone. I looked around. No one was to be seen. Then I heard a grunt. I struggled to get back into the room. But with certainty, I made it. I walked in the room. With the light from outside the room gazing in, I could now make out what the room looked like. I now regret trying to see it. I was correct. Odd shapes lay across the room. I could pick out the place to where I was laid down. The outline of my body was traced through the muck. Next to my outline was a body, with a blanket covered on top of it.

Not knowing if I should or not, I walked helplessly over to the body. Slowly, I pulled off the cover. Unbelievingly, I stepped back; it was Carlos. I breathed in deeply to relax my thoughts.

I knelt down to get a closer look. Someone bashed his head. Dried blood was running down his face. Then all of a sudden, he twitched, following with a grunt of pain. I helped him up. He was off balance the same way I was. I had him lean up against the wall until I was able to open the door farther. Then I half-carried him out of the room. With caution, we started to walk when someone grabbed my neck.

I tensed up and dropped my hand, making Carlos fall. Then the man picked him as well. He dragged us down the long hallway. The fast movements made my head spin. The question *What will happen?* hung in my brain.

As if we went on forever, we stopped. We came to a door that said, "Do not enter!" The man opened the door. I took a quick glance at Carlos.

We walked into a huge room. It was filled with chairs, a desk, and other miscellaneous items. His hands were still around our necks. He dragged us to the back of the room. There was a big curtain up against the wall. On the far right was a little pad that was, I guess, nailed to the wall. The man typed something in. Then the weirdest thing happened.

The curtain pulled apart, and a hidden door flung open. The man looked at us and tied a bandana around our eyes so we couldn't see. Then we continued on our walk.

At last, we came to a stop. The air was thick with smoke. Voices were all around Carlos and me. Finally, the bandanas were wiped off our faces. All that was in sight was a big long card table. About ten men were sitting around it, playing poker. The one at the end of the table looked up and smiled. He stood up. He had a navy blue jacket with a white shirt and tie underneath and a pair of dark navy blue pants. The rest of the group stood up as well. The man let go of our necks and bowed to show respect. Then he pushed us in the direction of the table.

"Thank you, X-ray. Now you may go," the man at the end of the table said. X-ray bowed once more and left the room. Then the man came and walked over to us. He rested his hands in front of him. "Natalie, at last we meet. I am Lar Mandel, the leader of the Mafia. Your parents talked about you often."

I look up at him. His eyes were dark with no feeling whatsoever. "Well, aren't you going to say anything?" he asked me.

I smiled. "Yeah, what do I have to do to get out of this joint? Clean up that room you put me in?" I asked.

The smile disappeared from his face. Mandel snapped his fingers twice, and two men came over from the table. One of them had lost his left eye at some point in his life because he had an eye patch on. Mandel called him Slash. The other was a heavier man who had a neck shaped of a piece of wood cut at a lumberyard. His name was Mulct (interesting name).

The two guys came over to him, and he said something to them in a different language. Then they walked over to us and held my arms. Then as if Mandel was at the gym, he punched me in the gut. But it was not hard. It was if he only did it to look good. I could tell that he had massive strength. But if he did, then why didn't he use it. Then Slash and Mulct dropped me. I got up. Carlos was doing nothing but stand there with his mouth open.

"Slash, take Natalie to the suite with her friend Carlos. They need to freshen up before dinner is served," Mandel suggested.

With that, Carlos and I were once again moved.

Slash showed us to the suite in silence. It was as if we were on a tour. We went up the stairs then downstairs. Finally, we came to a door that said "Private Suite." Slash took out a key from his pocket. He stuck it in the hole of the door to open it.

We walked inside. At first, I thought we were in a fairy tale. Slash looked at us, bowed, and then disappeared outside the door. Carlos was still uneasy on his feet. "This place is strange," I commented. "One part is filthy when the other is like a castle in a fairy tale."

Carlos nodded and sat down on the chair in front of him. I decided to look around. Two wall windows stretched from one end to the other. Then you would walk up a step, and that's where the beds were. Two king-size beds laid on the top level. One was on one end of the wall, and one was across from it on the other end.

Then came the time to look at the bathroom. I walked through the door to see a shower and a bathtub. I came out of the bathroom, anxious to tell Carlos, but when I caught sight of him, he was on the chair asleep. Since he was sleeping, I had a chance to think about our escape. Lar Mandel said that we would be joining him for dinner. Then when it got dark, he would be in bed. So then we would be able to escape. Wouldn't we? Or would they be like on TV and have video cameras all around the place?

Now at 7:30 p.m. I woke up Carlos so he could get dressed. An hour earlier, get this, a maid came in with a trunk of clothes for us to pick out. I was wearing a blue-and-white strapless dress. I wasn't much of a dress-type girl. But in these matters, I didn't have much of a choice, for two reasons. Number 1, that was all there was for me. Also, when the maid came and gave the clothes, she said that I was supposed to wear it.

When Carlos opened his eyes, he made an expression that could only mean one thing—he was surprised to see me in a dress. "Wow," he asked with sarcasm in his voice.

I walked over to my bed to fold my now dirty, used clothes. "Shut up. And there is a set of clothes for you to put on. So move yourself to the bathroom and get dressed, unless you want to be dressed as a salad when Lar Mandel hears that you didn't follow directions," I returned.

Half an hour went by, and a knock came from the door. I went to get it; it was the maid. She smiled as she looked at me in the dress. "Does it look okay?" I asked her.

She nodded. "You look much better than the other girls did when they were taken here," she complimented.

I gave a meaningless smile as I went to get Carlos off his butt from the chair. We walked out of the room. Carlos gave a childish smile to the maid as he went past her. As she closed the door, she rolled her eyes. "You two seem pretty upbeat even though you are going to dinner with a person you don't know," she analyzed.

I smiled while looking down at my feet, trying to keep my balance in these high heels. "Well, I'm just trying to, like, gather evidence that Lar Mandel killed my parents. And if I need to act like I like them, then I'll do it," I explained.

She looked at me like I crazy then slowly nodded her head. "Okay?"

I looked down at her feet. She was wearing heels as I did; she didn't seem to have any trouble walking. "Does that mean you would be willing to marry his son?"

I looked over at her with astonishment. "Marry his son? Lar Mandel has a son? Who?"

Carlos jogged up to keep in step with us. "Isn't anyone going to pay any attention to me?" he asked.

I didn't look back but put my finger up, meaning for him to keep quiet. "What's his name?" I asked again.

The maid sighed. "Alistair, and that's all I'm going to tell you," she said.

"But am I not too young to get married? After all, I am only sixteen."

"No, Lar Mandel's wife was fifteen years younger than him."

"Well, how old is this Alistair guy?"

"He is 17. But don't worry. You two would have at least a year to get to know each other."

Finally, we came to a double door. I looked back at Carlos; he was messing with his nails. "Yo, what on earth are you doing?" I asked him.

He shrugged his shoulders helplessly and said, "I'm nervous."

I shook my head in shame. If this was how it was going to go in there, I might as well kill myself now.

We walked in. As usual, there was a dim light. Straight ahead was a long table. At the end of it was Lar Mandel. He motioned us to come forward. The maid put her hand on my shoulder as if saying, "Good luck."

We walked toward him in an orderly fashion. Carlos walked next to me. I could feel that he was sweating. As soon as we about two feet away from him, he stood up. He went over, shook Carlos's hand, and motioned to where he should sit. Then he faced me. He smiled and took my hand as well. I thought he was going to shake it as he did to Carlos, but instead, he brought it up to his emotionless mouth and kissed it.

I nodded and sat down in the seat that was for me. Mandel then snapped his fingers, and out came two maids with food. They set down the food and left. Then Mandel motioned his hands upward, saying that we could begin to eat.

There were a multiple of forks and spoons. I looked to see what was on my plate—escargot. I never traveled to France, but I did know that escargot was snails. (Snails, I had tons of them back home in the yard. That was until my neighbor asked if he could have them, and now I know why. He eats them)

We started to eat when a knock came from the door. Mandel called, "Enter."

Then to obey, the door opened, and the maid from earlier came strolling in. "Alistair is here for dinner," she said.

He nodded. "Then show my son in!"

She gave a weak smile and left. I was almost jumping out of my seat. I was anxious to meet this Alistair in person. Besides, I should have a right. After all, if I was supposed to get married to him, I should know who he is.

We waited for a while when the door started to open. First, a hand showed, then the rest of the body. Finally, I could make out who it was. And when I did, I wanted to die . . .

CHAPTER 3

The man walked in as Mandel stood up. Then Mandel looked down upon me. I then stood up as well.

The man closed the door behind him. He then pulled out his derringer from inside his shirt, put in at the end of the table, and walked toward me.

He walked over with caution. "Miss Natalie," he said, bowing.

I looked at him with confused eyes as he brought my hand up to kiss it.

"Josh Brian," I asked, while putting my hand back in its original position.

"No, I am sorry for the confusion at the school a couple of *years* back. My real name is Alistair Mandel, and the man you are standing next to is my father."

I looked at the two. I could somewhat see the resemblance.

Mandel cleared his throat, "Yes well, I have assigned a room for you two so you get to know each other better."

I had to think about this for a moment. When you watch movies and someone says that a room was assigned so two people could get to know each other better, that normally meant . . . well, never mind.

I turned to look at him. "For what reason?" I asked with suspicion.

Mandel smiled while meeting eyes with Alistair. "Well, I think you two will be seeing each other quite often in the days to follow. Therefore, I would like you to get to know each other first. So go. Alistair, you know the room I'm talking about, don't you?" Mandel asked Alistair.

With that, Carlos walked over and patted my back as if trying to say, "See you in the long run." Then Alistair picked up his derringer and opened the door as he waited for me to follow.

I took one last look at everyone, as if saying good-bye for the last time. I walked past Alistair on the way out. Then I was stuck with him.

Mandel closed the door that was left open. Then he walked over, sat down in his chair, and continued eating with Carlos as they did only a couple of minutes ago.

Carlos looked up at Mandel, "Do you think everything will be okay?"

Mandel leaned his arms on the table to speak. "Look, son, if I know you brother, Alistair will be fine," he said, comforting Carlos.

Carlos sighed. "I wasn't talking about Alistair, Father; I was talking about Natalie. I really care about her, and if anything happens to her, I'll feel responsible."

Mandel made a confused expression. "Why should you feel responsible?"

Once again, Carlos sighed. "Well, I'll feel that I should have told her the truth about you being my real father and Alistair, my brother."

Mandel looked at Carlos with a serious face. "Carlos, am I going to have a problem with you?"

"Of course not. Why would you?"

Mandel shrugged his shoulders as he popped a sliced apple into his mouth. "Well, you know what I'll have to do to you if you start to talk; don't you?" Mandel said as if trying to scare his son.

Carlos nodded. "Of course, Father. You should be worrying about Alistair. I'm the one who has the Mafia blood in me. Alistair is just like mother. By the way, do you even like Natalie?"

Mandel looked down and scratched his eyebrow. "Yes, I do. It was a shame for her parents' death. I liked them very much. That is why I decided for her to come and live here."

Carlos put on his most famous confused face that made him look like a donkey. "But I thought you killed her parents?"

Mandel shook his head. "Heck, no. I cherished her parents very much. They were one of my best." There was fear in his eyes. "I wouldn't kill one of my men. However, my brother would."

That was the end of that discussion.

I walked through the halls with Alistair in silence. I would look over at him occasionally with innocent eyes. Then he would look at me while I looked away. Finally, I expressed, "What are we doing?"

He looked over at he surprised of my tone. "I don't know. What do you want to do? We would play cards," he said with sarcasm.

I laughed. "Very funny. No, I'm serious, Alistair, sir, person. What do we need a room for?"

He looked at me. "Are you serious? You don't know why my father gave us a room to be alone?"

I now knew what he was getting at—sex. I stepped back. "Now, look, I think you're a great guy, but I'm not going to have sex with you."

Alistair held up his derringer and pulled the cartridge so you could see the ammo. Then he snapped it back in. Then as if he knew me forever, he picked up his shirt just enough to put the gun back.

We walked in silence for a very long time. That was until Alistair stopped. We stopped in front of a door. As usual, he brought out a key. He then opened the door and allowed me to go first. As I walked in, I would swear that he swayed his hand across my back. He came in as well and closed the door behind him.

Like the other room, it was big, but there was only one bed. On top of it were pajamas for me and a pair of shorts with T-shirt for Alistair. I sat down on the bed to see a book on top of the nightstand. I picked it up and started to read the back.

I read the first couple of pages; they weren't very interesting. "Just to let you know, I don't wanna do it with you. I'm not that kind of guy," Alistair said out of nowhere.

I looked over at him. "What did you say?" I asked in astonishment.

"You know what I said. I am not going to repeat myself. You are too beautiful. That was my father's idea. I just wanted you to know that."

In addition to what he said, he grabbed his shorts and the T-shirt and headed into the bathroom to change. When he came out, he said, "You can have the bed, I'll take the couch."

Before I could say anything, a knock came from the door. I looked at him as if he was to go and get it. "I'm not exactly dressed right to get the door. They might think that . . ." He did not have to finish his sentence for I knew what he was getting at.

Why wasn't he dressed correctly? He was in shorts.

I walked over to the door and opened it. There was Slash standing while smiling a suspicious smile like a child would if he took cookies out of the cook jar when he was not supposed to.

"Mr. Mandel would like to see you," he announced.

I looked at Alistair. There he was on the couch with a cover over himself as if he were freezing cold. "It'll be all right," he said.

Therefore, I went. I closed the door behind me and followed him. As we were walking through the halls, Slash looked at me. "So how do like it here so far?" he asked.

"What do you mean?" I asked.

"Well, normally when we have visitor, they want to talk so we need to get rid of them."

A mental picture entered my brain. "How do you exactly get rid of them?"

"Well, it all depends on how bad they are. I might have to cut their neck and leave them there to bleed to death. Or I would give them the apache torture where I make to fires side by side and put two stacks in front of the fires then I would tie their wrists to the stacks and let their hands burn away."

I made a wincing sound.

He looked over at me. "You don't believe me, do you? You think we're that bad. The Mafia's not murderers. Well, not normally. You don't have to worry about that. Mandel loves you."

I wanted to say something else, but we came to another door. He knocked on the door and a yell of "Enter" came to follow.

He opened the door and nodded for me to go in.

I walked toward the door and waved back at Slash before going in. Then without any warning, I pushed myself forward. I walked in and closed the door behind me.

I strained to breathe for I was nervous as ever. The light was dim, and I couldn't make out where Mandel was. Then all of a sudden, a hand reached out and touched my shoulder.

I plunged forward while doing a double reverse hip throw. I stood up quickly to see whom I dodged. Fortunately, it was only Mandel. On the other hand, unfortunately. He held out his hand as if trying to steady me.

I stood up with a somewhat embarrassed expression on my face. Mandel smiled as he walked over and turned on a switch that made the room light up more. I could now see clearly.

"Natalie, how nice of you to come as I requested. How about we go somewhere that is less polluted, shall we?" he said.

We made our way down the hall and up a staircase. I looked down at my feet. I couldn't help looking at the tiled flooring. Blue, white, blue, white. The pattern kept repeating itself as if there was no end.

We turned to the left, and Mandel stopped in front of a door that was different from the others. This door was arched while painted with a dark stain (still wood, but a tint darker).

He opened it up. "I thought our conversation could be held in the lounge," he said as he walked in and flickered on the florescent lights. "Please sit down."

I did as he asked and sat down at the nearest chair. He stayed standing and paced back and forth in front of me. "Please let me start by apologizing from earlier at dinner. I had no reason to hit you."

I looked down. "You got mad. You didn't know what you were doing," I replied. "Besides, I learned how to take pain."

He looked at me. "Oh, may I ask where?"

I stood up as he was. "A couple of years ago. Before my parents were part of the Mafia, they were part of the CIA. While they were in training, they taught me a little too. But not a lot. But then the CIA got my parents stressed so they decided to go against them and join up with you."

Mandel looked away as if he were surprised at my explanation. "I had no idea that you trained with the CIA. I was once with the CIA, if you didn't know."

To act impressed, I looked at him with surprised expression. "Cool. Please tell me about it."

"Well, when I was no older than you now, my parents died. So my Uncle Ian gave me up and gave me to the headman, or in other words, he gave me to the man who was running the CIA at that time, Andrew Thompson. There he taught me everything there is to know about defending myself. But as you can see, I have gotten at bit rusty. Then I was sent on a mission, and they let me down and did not come and help me when the Mafia captured me.

Where I stayed and joined up with them to hopefully get revenge of the CIA in the future. And look at me now. I'm the head of it."

I nodded and then turned to look around the room. It was big, like all of them. But something was different about this one. I did not know what. I felt as if we were being watched.

"Now, let's get down to business. Shall we?"

I nodded in agreement, and we both sat down at a table. "I would like to start," Mandel said. "I would like you to know that I have nothing to do with your parents' death. I know that you don't believe that now. But I hope that by the end of the next few weeks, you can see me telling the truth; and hopefully you can see me as your future father-in-law."

I dropped my mouth open. "What?" I asked.

"I would like it very much if you and Alistair would get married. He cares for you deeply."

I sighed. "I will have to think about it. And I will get back to you soon."

He smiled. I could see that it was a strain for him to do so. It was as if there was something in his mind which was covering up his false emotions. "Splendid. Oh, one other thing. Well will be moving to a better house tomorrow. In Malta, in fact. Nevertheless, I think you will be up by then. We will be leaving around 3:00 p.m.," he said.

I nodded while getting up. "Thank you for this chat. It makes me feel better about what has happened in the last couple of days. Or hours."

I started to move out of the room when I stopped in my tracks. "Could it be possible that I might be able to see Carlos tomorrow?" I asked

He smiled, but this time, it was sincere. "Of course. I will have him come up to you at eleven."

"But will he know which room it is?"

"Oh, yes, he knows this place very well. Good night."

With his remark, I led myself out of the room.

I walked back to my room, thinking about what he said. "I hope that by the end of the next couple of weeks, you will think of me as telling the truth, and maybe you could call me your father-in-law."

I know that these were not his exact words, but it still means the same. When he said that by the end of the next couple of weeks,

I would think of him as telling the truth, he must have thought that I didn't believe him. And if that was not the reason, then why would he be so foolish to say that I can trust him? Could it be the situation that I'm in? He thinks that I cannot believe anyone now from still being in shock.

Another thing. He said that Carlos knew this place well. An answer came to my head admittedly, but I blocked it just as fast as it came to me. Then I let it return to make sure that it was not possible. Could Lar Mandel be Carlos's real father? Could Alistair and Carlos be brothers? What did Carlos do after I left with Alistair? Did he stay and chat with Mandel?

I decided not to worry about it. If it were true about Carlos, he would have told me.

I came to my room. I opened the door. When I walked in, I was stunned to see Alistair up, reading about kitty cats.

I walked over the couch in which he was lying. "What are you doing?" I asked while laughing. Alistair was having apple juice and with his white T-shirt and plaid shorts. It looked like an episode of *AFV* (*America's Funniest Home Videos*). Only in this case, it would be *MFV* (*Mafia's Funniest Home Videos*).

He smiled, "Reading. How was the talk with my father?"

I sat down in the chair beside him. "Don't you mean 'your father' but 'my father-in-law'?"

He looked up at me with eyes of disbelief. "Your father-in-law?"

I nodded while sighing. "Yes, so sometime this week, you are to announce your engagement to me. Or sometime."

Alistair gasped. "So I'm getting married to you?"

I looked at him. He was cute, funny, smart, and dangerous. Well, not dangerous, but very fit if he ever had to defend himself. From the look of his arms, he must be going to the gym at least every other day.

I shrugged my shoulders. "That's the general drift of it. But I don't think he meant that we have to get married just as yet."

He exhaled. "Thank goodness. I mean, I love . . . I always loved you. Only I don't think I want to get married right now. Maybe next year. What do you think?"

I exhaled as well but in astonishment. He loved me. I had never heard those words before. Well I did; but never did I hear those words come from a boy's mouth. (He is only seventeen. How could he really love someone? He's so young he doesn't even probably know what that word really means. With only talking to him for about a couple of hours, I do not know how he could *love* me already.)

I nodded to his question of whatever it was and got up. I walked over to the bed and picked up my pajamas on my way to the bathroom to change.

I came out in my pink tank top and pink frog pajama pants. I walked over, grabbed a book, and sat down on the bed. I was reading *How to Say No.* I read a couple of pages when I looked over at Alistair. He was sitting or lying on the couch. I watched him as he would occasionally pick up his cover that would fall down on the floor. I pitied him.

I went into the walk-in closet and pulled out the phone to the house cleaner's room. "Hello, would you please bring up two mugs of hot coco?" I asked.

The maid who was on the other line said that they would be up in about five minutes with the coco. I looked around in the closet. A couple of hours ago, this place was empty. Now, it was filled with clothes.

The maid came at the time she told me she would. I took the two coco mugs from her and thanked her. I walked her to the door then went back to Alistair. I sat down and gave him the coco.

"Do you want some?" I asked. I went back up and went over to the chair beside him. "What are you doing?" I said, again trying to get his attention.

He took it but in silence. I didn't know what to say. Why was he being so quiet? Then all of a sudden, he started laughing. I looked over at him with an obvious expression on my face. "Why are you laughing?" I asked.

He looked up at me and stopped. "Why do you want to know?" he sassed. I hoped he was using sarcasm, but from the expression on his face, about forty-five percent of my hopes were wrong.

I looked at him and wet my lips in disappointment. I look over at the clock hanging on the wall near my bed. Ten twenty-three in the evening was what it said. I guess it wouldn't be that bad of a time to go to bed. With that, I started to get up.

Suddenly a clammy hand, obviously from sweating, grabbed my own and pulled me back down. I sat down without ease. I looked at him with no emotion in my face. He gave me a faint smile.

"I'm sorry, I didn't mean to sound harsh. I'll tell you the reason I was laughing if you stay up a little longer," he pleaded.

I sighed. "Well, I guess it wouldn't hurt for me to stay up a little longer," I replied.

"Well, when I was little, my father would always say that when a girl got you hot coco and sat down next to you, it meant that they like you."

I looked down a little embarrassed from his comment. Not a second in between, I replied with "Well, I guess your father was right." I know that what I said might have sounded a little bit, well, *lovey-dovey*, if you want to call it, but hey, it's my story, I can put what I want in it.

He looked at me with soft, gentle eyes. Then without any notice, he put his hand up against my chin and dragged it to his and . . .

I won't tell you the rest for a very good reason. I don't want to tell you. Besides, to continue my story, I'll have to tell you anyway.

So yes, we were kissing when the door opened. We didn't exactly notice. Well, we didn't until a "Ah, well, I'm glad you're getting along" came from behind the door.

We came away from each other and looked at the person who spoke; it was Mandel. "Oh, we were just saying good night," I assured him. *Weren't we?* I was never kissed like that. I wondered what they're both thinking.

I got up from my seat and stood there, hoping to have an innocent expression on my face. "Yes, well, like I said, I'm glad that you two are getting along. As for that, I will go to bed. Good night," he said.

I walked him to the door. He smiled before he left the room. I leaned on the door to close it. I turned around and headed back to my seat.

There was an awkward silence. The kind you see in a movie before everyone starts talking at once. I looked up over at him. He was staring at the wall, not doing anything. "I hope you understand that that kiss didn't mean anything," I said without warning.

He looked at me. "I know. It was cold without any feeling. I'm sorry. I shouldn't have kissed you," he replied.

I looked at him with sorrow in my eyes. Why was he saying this? Did he mean it? With his rude and surprising comment, I made myself to the light switch. "Good night," I said as I flipped it off and clumsily headed for my bed.

Even in the dark, I could see him clearly. He had his derringer. He was looking at it funny. As if he was going to use it. I didn't know what to make of him. At first, he's hot and anything that any girl would want, but then no more than a second later, he was like a terrorist who was meaner than the devil itself. On the other hand, was it just me?

It took me a long time to get to sleep. I could tell it was the same for Alistair. I would hear him toss and turn. I didn't know what was going to happen tomorrow. All I could do was pray and hope that it would be better than today.

CHAPTER 4

The morning sun woke me up from my night's rest. The curtains were away from the windows, and the room was like empty. I looked over to see if Alistair was up. He was gone. I turned my head to see if the door to the bathroom was closed. For if it was, that would mean that he was in. Nevertheless, it was wide open.

I got out of bed to go get dressed. I made my bed before I made my way to the walk-in closet. When I came close enough to reach out and grab the doorknob, I heard voices. "Don't take her away from me," a boy said. It sounded like Carlos.

"Why not? You'll just destroy her when you get tired of her anyway," a voice sounding like Alistair replied.

"Just stay away from her; she's not for you."

"On the contrary, we had a good discussion last night. So just buzz off."

Very quietly, I opened the door just so I could see who really was in. I was right; it was Carlos and Alistair. I closed the door and walked away.

As soon as I started to walk away, the door opened and the two boys came out. "Oh, Natalie, you're up," said Carlos.

I spun around, a little embarrassed to be *seen* in my pajamas. Alistair looked at me up and down. "Nice frogs," he complimented.

I didn't know if he was kidding or what, but all I did was push through the two to make way for myself to go the closet to get my clothing.

I came out of the dressing room with a blue tank top and tan shorts on. I walked over to the bed to see if everything was in order. I grabbed my sweatshirt and headed out the door. Just as I opened it, Carlos and Alistair ran in. They knocked me down.

I was on the ground, not exactly collecting what just happened. I looked up to see Carlos on top on me; no wonder I couldn't breathe. Alistair pulled him off and helped me up.

"Sorry about that," Alistair said. "But our . . ." He stopped while looking over at Carlos. "I mean, my father says that there was a slight change in our plans and we will be flying over in about one hour."

While explaining to me what was going on, they made their way to the sofa. "So what do you want to do?" Carlos asked. "We have an hour."

I looked at him and shrugged my shoulders. "I don't know. What can you do around here?" I questioned.

Carlos looked over at Alistair. "Well, we can go swimming, riding, tennis, watch a movie, sit here and talk, or shopping," he replied.

My mouth dropped open. "You have a pool."

Alistair laughed. "Yep, and a tennis court and riding stables."

I put my hands up to rest them on my head. "Then why in the world are you moving?"

"This place is so small" was his answer.

I was so confused. They had everything, and they still wanted to move to a bigger house. Something was wrong with this picture.

"How about we talk? Now, hum. What do you want to talk about," Carlos opened up.

I looked at him and then smiled. "Okay, let's talk about you. For some reason, I don't think you are who you are, if you know what I mean."

He sighed then said, "Oh, great. Now we have Nancy Drew with us" under his breath.

"How did you know this place around here so well unless you've been here before? Besides, why are you always with Alistair? It's as if you've known him for a long time. So are you going to give me answers? Or let me continue with my analysis?"

He looked over at Alistair. I knew that I got them now. "Well, okay. Alistair and I are brothers."

The whole night, I have been practicing for that answer, but even with practice, it still came as a bit of a shock. "Why didn't you tell me this years ago," I asked with sadness in my voice. "You lied to me for the past ten years."

I got up and headed for the door. I stopped before I opened it then turned my head toward them. "You betrayed me. I thought you were my friend." With that last comment, I made my way out the door.

Carlos just sat there. He had shame in his eyes. "Look what you did," Alistair budded in. "See how you made her feel. You said that everything would be okay. Ha!"

Then he got up as well. "You better go talk to her. I'm not. It's you turn." Then he left as well.

Carlos sat there as he did the last ten minutes, confused. *Why was she mad at me?* he asked himself. *I didn't do anything. All I did was what my father told me to do,* he thought.

After consulting with himself about with what he should do, he got up and headed out the door like Alistair and I did in the last fifteen minutes.

I walked down the hallway, not thinking about where I was going. I came to a door. Just as I was about to open it, it swung open. Out came Mandel. "Well, Natalie, is something wrong?" he asked me with caution as he put something in his pocket.

I looked at him and then blinked a couple of times. "Oh, no. Sorry for bothering you. I was just walking, I guess," I answered him.

He smiled. "Well, perhaps you wouldn't mind taking a walk with me."

He turned and started to walk. Slowly, I turned to follow him. "Was there something you wanted?" I asked as I came into step with him.

"No, well, yes, I wanted to talk to you about something."

I cleared my throat to tell him to continue. When that didn't work, I said, "And what did you want to talk to me about."

"Oh, yes, well, we're going to be going back to Malta in a couple minutes, and I wanted to talk to you about what your place with be like."

"So you want to tell me what my house is going to look like."

He gave a little chuckle. "No, my dear. You are so funny, but no. When I say 'your place,' I mean your position in the Mafia."

"So you want me to work?"

"Yes and no. When I say work, I mean well . . ." He didn't continue but sighed.

"You know, in a royal family. There's the king and queen. Then the prince and princess. And then the lord and lady. And so on. They all have their own place in the royal family. That's what I mean when I say you place. Now, do you understand," he explained.

I smiled. "Oh, yeah. Sorry, I got a little blond there," I said.

He smiled while looked up at my chocolate colored hair. "Now back to what I was saying. Your place would be like the princess's. You could do whatever you want. Because well I am the king. In other words, I'm the ruler on the organization. And then it's Alistair then *you* and then Carlos."

"Why is Carlos last?"

"He messed up in the past. He's not ready to be second in command. Now do you have any questions?"

"Yes. Do you have any other son than Alistair?"

All of a sudden, his smile was off his face and he became serious. "No, I do not."

"You're a liar. Carlos is you other son," I joked.

He smiled. "How did you know?"

I looked up at him. "Dude, you just like told me. Plus, I sort of figured it out."

"You know, I like you."

With his comment, he came up, kissed my forehead, and was about to open the door that we came to. Then before he left to go, he looked back. "I'm glad about how fast you fit in. You act as if you have been with us forever. I'm glad."

Then when he was about to open the door, in came Carlos. "You never told me that she was smart," Mandel said to him as he left the room.

"Yeah, sorry about that," Carlos answered back.

I gave him half a smile. "What do you want," I asked.

Carlos waited for the door to close. "I want to apologize. I had no reason to lie to you."

"You were keeping a secret from me."

Carlos just nodded.

"I have one more question for you. If Mandel's your dad, then who were those people whom you lived with all of these years?"

He sighed. "My aunt and uncle. They knew that I would be going back to my father."

Then it all became clear to me. "Oh, now I get it. When you came into my house after school that one time and said that the Mafia was after us, you only did that so you could come home. Besides, they really did want to some answers answered. They wanted to know if I would marry Mandel's son. This means that you'll be my brother-in-law."

He smiled. "Looks like it, sis."

This was a very corny/stupid moment for me. I smiled as well then for some odd reason, we hugged (for no odd reason). Then we both saw Alistair make his way up the hall toward us. "Well, I'm glad to see that you two are getting along again," he said as he put his hand around my shoulder. "It's time to go. Well, I mean it's time to get on the plane."

Therefore, we *all* made our way to the front door. "How are we going to get to the air port?" I asked. And I realized that even without him asking me, Alistair and I were now going out.

Alistair looked at me. "Well, you go out the door, down the steps, and into the plane. I don't think we are going to an airport, are we, Carlos?" he said.

"No. I think Father said that it would too much of a pain so he ordered a private jet," Carlos said.

My mouth dropped open as the guys pulled me out of the house and onto the plane. Trust me, it wasn't easy. Well, I shouldn't say plane; it was a jet. It was a big jet too. Bigger than me (ha-ha).

A couple of minutes later, Mandel came in. He decided to sit in the far front away from us (I can't really blame him).

Soon, we heard a loud sound, and we were off. As we started to take off, our ears popped (not very good).

After five minutes of flying, I got bored. Alistair and Carlos were across from me, having arm wrestling matches.

"Why are you two doing that?" I asked as I walked over to the seat next to them.

"I don't know," they both said at the same time.

"Yeah, okay," I said as I made my way back to my original seat.

Once I was about two feet away from my seat, the plane shifted to the right and everyone fell and hit the floor.

CHAPTER 5

The plane was going this way and that. Everyone was on the floor. I looked up and shook my head. I then started to get up but couldn't. Something was wrong with my right leg.

I tried to get up again, but the same results came; nothing happened. I could hear Mandel yell for Carlos and Alistair to go see what was happening in the cockpit. Then he ran over to me, noticing that I wasn't up yet.

"Are you okay?" he asked with ease.

"I can't move my right leg," I winced.

He nodded while moving his hand down my leg. Then he pushed in different spots (very awkward). Then he asked me if it hurt. I nodded while wincing in pain. "It's definitely fractured. I can't do much more until we get to Malta. That is if we ever do get there," he assured.

Then he picked me up without any trouble and laid me on the seat that I wanted to go to a couple of minutes before.

After he put me down, he headed for the cockpit. Soon, all I could hear was yelling. "What are you doing here? How did you get in here? Get off the plane!" I could hear Mandel yelling. "I don't know or care how you are to get off. You got on, you can get off. Jump with a parachute. On the other hand, you could jump without one. I don't care. Look, I have Natalie Maclusta in there. *And* she is going to become my daughter-in-law someday. And I don't want her to get confused."

Who was in there that I would get confused about? Then I just realized that I started to like him as a father-in-law (oh, brother). Nevertheless, the whole reason I came here was to bust him. Nevertheless, if he really liked me, then why would he kill my parents? There has to be an explanation. Maybe he didn't kill mom and dad. However, if he did not, then who did?

As soon as I came back to reality, I heard yelling once more. "Let me meet this smart pretty girl that you are talking about," an unusual voice said.

"No, I won't let you," Alistair yelled.

"Maybe it's best, son. Then if she ever does meet up with him, she'll know who it is," Mandel said.

Soon, I saw Carlos come out with Alistair. Nevertheless, Mandal didn't show. "Where's Father, I mean, Mandel?" I asked.

Before one of the boys could answer, out came Mandel. But someone came behind him. It was him, two of him. Wait, was that even possible? The Mandel who came out first said, "This is my twin brother. Who in fact is also Lar Mandel. But we call him M2. And yes, it might get a little confusing at times. In other words, he's the evil brother," the real Mandel said. (Well, not real, but the one, well, Mandel #1.)

I nodded in confusion and terror. M2 looked at me with evil eyes, as if he was planning something. "What did you do to your leg?" M2 asked.

"I hurt it by falling when the plane shifted. Do you have any other pathetic questions I can answer for you?" I sassed.

He started to lunge toward me, but Alistair stepped in front. "She's not as stupid as you thought, is she?" he said.

He grunted. "I'll be back," he murmured. After that, he left to the cockpit and disappeared.

Mandel looked at me. "I don't think he likes you very much," he guessed.

"Ah, no biggie. I don't like him very much either," I said while smiling.

The three of them sat down again while chuckling to my last comment. Alistair sat next to me, and Carlos sat across from us. Even Mandel sat with us. "Hey, Dad, guess Natalie called you," Alistair said.

Mandel smiled at me. "What did she call me?" he asked.

I nudged Alistair in the chest to make him shut up. "She called you 'Father.'"

Mandel looked at me as if waiting for an explanation. "It just slipped out. Sorry, I'll call you Mandel from now on," I explained.

He smiled. "No, no. That is okay. I like you calling me 'Father.' Thank you."

I smiled at him. "So how long until we reach Malta?"

Carlos answered, "Well, in about ten minutes."

I nodded. "How is Natalie going to get off the jet? Can she walk," Alistair asked his father.

"She fractured it so of course, she can't walk on it. One of us can carry her. She is so light," Mandel said.

"I'll carry her," Alistair said.

"Well, I better go and revive the pilots that Mandel #2 knocked out. Good thing that the jet was on automatic flying.

Therefore, Mandel went and got them awake. After that, it was smooth-flying, thank goodness.

Soon, the jet was landing. Just as it did when it was taking off, our ears popped.

We came to a stop. Mandel went out first then Carlos. Then Alistair came over and picked me up with no problem at all, and we headed out after them.

We came off the plane. There was a wheelchair waiting for me at the bottom of the steps. Alistair put me in it and asked me if I knew how to move in it. I said that I did.

Once we were on the black top, a whole pile of men in gray and black suits came toward us.

Mandel shook hands and laughed with them. Finally, he brought them over to where I was. "This is Natalie Maclusta. She will be living with us from now on. She will become my daughter-in-law. Well, I hope one of these days anyway," he said.

I looked up at everyone and made a shy smile. "Hello," I said.

"Good afternoon, young lady," a man said. The only thing that I could get out of him was that his name was Yassen Bicker. He was in a black suit. Obviously very expensive. His hair was fair, brown, and short. He had a round face. His eyes were almost hollow. "I see you hurt yourself."

I nodded while trying to act mature. "Yes, sir, I fell."

He nodded as well. "Well, Natalie, I think we better get you home," Mandel suggested.

"Oh, yes, thank you."

Then he came behind me, took the handles from the wheelchair, and drove me away. Carlos and Alistair followed us. It was almost as if they were princes. The men got out of their way in a flash. "I don't think he likes me very much, "I told Mandel as we left the area.

"It's okay; you'll get to know him. He is like my best friend. Are you hungry?" he said.

"Well, I could eat, but I don't have to."

"Good. When we get home, we came have dinner."

"Dinner," I asked confused

"Oh, sorry, I mean, supper."

"Oh. I'll have to get used to this."

He laughed and patted my shoulder.

Soon, we came to a very big building. Then Alistair came over and picked me up out of the wheelchair. I didn't know what he was doing, but I thought I asked enough questions for right now.

Soon, a limo came up and around the curb. My mouth dropped open. Then another followed. "How many do you need?" I asked, forgetting not to ask more questions.

"Well, one is for Father, and the other one is for Carlos, you and me. Why, do you want one for yourself?" he stated.

"No, no. One limo is enough for me."

A man got out of one of limos and opened the back door. I couldn't take my eyes off him. He had a driver's suit with a hat to top it all off.

"I'll be going in this one. You three will meet me at the house. It'll take about two hours to get there. But I was wondering if one of you could go with me to keep me company. Natalie, would you care to join me?" he asked.

I didn't know what to say. "Yeah, I guess," I answered.

He smiled. "Great." Then he came over took me from Alistair and carried me over to the limo that he was going to be using. "Easy does it," he said as he sat me in the car.

He closed the door. Before he left to get in on the other side, he walked over toward Alistair and Carlos. "Now I want you to come straight home. M2 has a plan up his sleeve. And I want us all to be there for it. Do you understand me?"

He didn't wait for his sons to answer but hurried over and got into the other side of the limo. Without waiting, the two boys got in the limos in split-second timing.

Inside the limo was cooler than I could explain with words. There were two long seats, a table in the middle, a TV, and a sky window. There was silence for a long time.

"Are you ready to become part of the Mafia?" Mandal said finally.

I didn't exactly know what to say. He just asked me if I would want to become one of them. "You want me to become a terrorist and kill people?" I asked.

He looked at me, surprised. "Well, I wouldn't call it killing. Well, yeah, we do kill people. But only when we have to. You see, what the Mafia does is basically doing others' dirty work. And they pay us good money. But if they don't pay us, they end up being our next victims. But we also just have our own thing going on most of the time."

"Look, Mandal, Father. I always wanted to follow my parent's footsteps, but this sounds a little extreme. I'll have to think about it."

He smiled. "No, no. I think you get the wrong idea. Do you think you'll have to kill?"

"Yeah, isn't that the point?"

"No, not at all. When I asked you to become part of the Mafia, I didn't mean that you would take part in the things. You would be Alistair's girlfriend, and that automatically makes you one of us. But you would only carry the name as being part of the Mafia. Sort of like a secretary. You're part of whatever you're doing or helping, but you don't take part in it."

"So I would be like a secretary?"

"Oh, no. You would be much more important. People would know your name all over Europe. Everyone would respect you. They would nod their head in respect. You would rule. So how about it?"

I sighed then dazed off while looking away. "Well, I know I am going to regret this later, but . . . okay. I will become part of the Mafia."

He smiled. "Oh, good. Because if you wouldn't, they would kill you."

My mouth dropped open. "Kill me. Why?"

Now he sighed. "Because you would be staying with me, or us. In addition, you would hear all of our plans. And they would think that you would tell on us so they would keep you quiet by killing you."

"What a way to keep me quiet."

He laughed. "I really like you. When Alistair told me about you, I thought, 'Oh, no. Now who did my son find?' But now, I really like you."

I didn't really know how to reply. "Oh, well, thank you. I think."

"Yes, well, when we get to the house, you will have some paperwork to fill out."

"To be in the Mafia?"

"No, you're starting the work. You have to fill out some personnel files."

"You're going to have me working?"

"Well, yeah, like once a month. Can't you stand that?"

"Well, yeah. Okay."

We didn't talk for the rest of the ride there. I tried looking out of the window, but with them being tinted, I don't think I had a chance.

It was so quiet. So I thought I would think . . .

To start, I will talk about Mandel. It is hard for me to say this, but I do not; he's as bad as it seems. I thought back a couple of days ago. Well two years ago, someone around this joint killed my parents. Then just now, I headed out to find who killed them, but in doing so, I ended up at one of the people who I thought killed them. I am ashamed to admit it, but ever since they have died, I have been so happy. With Alistair, and Mandel (and Carlos, but he does not count because I will always have him).

All of a sudden, I came out of my thinking mode/daydream because the window came down. I could now see outside. The grass was green, and the sky was blue like I have never seen. It was beautiful.

CHAPTER 6

Finally, we got there. We came to two big gates. They looked old and *cool*. Soon, the driver got out of the car and went up to a little hole in the pole on the gate. "Mandel and Miss Natalie are here," he said.

Then he got back into the limo, and the gates magically opened. I watched with my mouth open. Mandel looked over at me and laughed quietly. "Welcome home," he told me.

"This is home?" I asked in a daze.

"Yep, it even has a pool, small arcade, riding stables, golf course, tennis court, and much more, but I forgot."

"How much did this cost?"

He smiled. "It's best not to ask questions."

I smiled, a little embarrassed. "I guess you're right. Sorry."

We went up a long driveway. It felt like it was an unending road. Finally, we came to a big, and I mean *big* house. Three stories high. They had three fountains outside with a huge garden. Mandel told me not to get out of the limo for someone would come over and open it for me. (Can you imagine it?)

And not for the first time, but he was right. A man came over and opened the door for me. I got out while leaning on anything that was around. Mandel then got out as well and said something in a different language.

Then a pair of crutches came out, brought by a man in long black pants and a white shirt. He gave them to me, bowed, and then said, "Miss."

I smiled while bowing my head slightly to show thank you. I put the crutches on and waited for Mandal to tell me what to do. "You go ahead in," Mandel told me. "The maids will show you around."

I nodded as two ladies in white dresses and black aprons came out and motioned me to follow them. "This way, miss," they finally said.

I followed them with interest. They showed me every room in the house. Finally, they took me to my room. "This room will be yours, miss. If you have any problems, just ring the bell, and someone will be with you directly."

She left the room with me in it all alone. I looked around. How did people get so much money? I swear, it looked like the Buckingham Palace. I wouldn't be surprised if it was.

I went over to the bed and pressed my hands on it to see how soft is was. *Not that bad,* I said to myself.

"Who are you talking to?" a voice said from behind me.

I spun around to see who it was. Naturally, it was Alistair. "Why do you do that?" I asked as I went over to look at the pile of suitcases that were lying on the floor. "Whose are these?"

Alistair blocked out that question and focused on the first one. "Why do I do what?"

I got up from the floor and looked over at the other end of the room while answering him. "You always sneak up on people?"

"No, I don't. Do I?"

I stopped everything that I was doing and looked at him. "Yeah," I said sassily.

He shrugged his shoulders as if he did not care. "Well, whatever. Sorry about that."

He started to walk toward the door. "By the way, those suitcases are for you," he said before he closed the door behind him. Then I guessed he forgot something because he opened it again. "Dinner will be at 6:00 p.m. sharp," he said before he closed the door again.

I scratched my hand on my head in confusion. Then forgot about that and continued on what I was doing a couple of minutes before—looking around.

I walked back over to the huge pile of suitcases on the floor. There was clothing but no closet. How does that work?

I thought about this for a little while. Then I looked around another ten minutes, looking for a closet. There was nothing. No door; nothing. I walked over and sat down on the bed to think. Should I go and ask Alistair if he knows?

Even though I did not want to, my brain told my legs to move. (This is totally off-topic, but did you ever notice how independent your brain is these days? It is amazing.)

Without being enthusiastic, I walked over to the door. I opened it and went out to the hall. I started to walk down the hall. If I knew Alistair well enough, he would be downstairs arguing with Carlos. However, the problem was that I hardly knew Alistair at all.

I walked over to the staircase. I put my hand on the handle and started to walk down. It was a very soft staircase (I am not kidding).

Everything was perfect until I noticed that I forgot to bring my crutches. Then I went down a step. I hit my leg on the pole and started to fall.

Everything was happening so fast. I tripped and went falling down a two-flight staircase. (Not what I would call enjoyable.)

Finally, I reached the bottom. However, I cannot tell you what happened afterward.

I woke up in my bed. My head hurt and then my leg. I could hear Carlos, Alistair, and Mandel all around, yelling. "She could have been badly hurt," I heard Carlos yell.

"Yeah, but she wasn't," Alistair said right after.

"Guys, settle down. The important thing is that she'll be okay," Mandel said.

I opened my eyes. At first, it was all just a blur. When my eyes came into focus, I could see Carlos and Alistair leaning on opposite sides of the bed, glaring at each other.

"Well, Natalie, you're up," Mandal said, trying to get Alistair and Carlos to settle down.

I tried to sit up, but I did not have enough strength. "What's going on?" I asked, puzzled.

"You had a bad fall, and this time, you really did hurt your leg. You'll have to stay in bed for the next few days to make sure it heals okay. Then you can get up and wear a cast," Mandel explained.

"Yeah, but you wouldn't have fallen if *someone* was with you," Carlos said while looking over at Alistair.

I looked over at Alistair, waiting to see if he had anything to add to Carlos's comment.

Finally, he said something, but it was not what I thought he would say. "I'll be waiting outside," Alistair said as he made his way to the door.

"Good, maybe she'll be safe without you," Carlos yelled after him.

Mandel slammed his hand down on the nightstand next to my bed. "That is enough, Carlos. You do not speak to you brother like that," he yelled.

Carlos made a sassy smile. "You can't do anything to me," he told his father.

"Oh, I'm afraid I could do quite a lot. Now leave."

With his father's comment, Carlos left. As he was walking toward the door, Mandel added, "Just remember, son, your brother has more power than you do, and one of these days, he just might want to use it."

Carlos slammed the door behind him. Mandel looked back at me. "Don't worry about him," he said.

I looked confused. "Carlos?" I asked.

"No, Alistair. You know when he said that he would wait outside the door. He thinks that it's his fault that you got hurt."

"He thinks this is his fault? Why?"

Mandel looked down. "Because he was supposed to bring you downstairs to have someone look at your leg, but when he came down, you weren't with him. So right when we were coming down the hall to go up and get you, we heard a big bang and came running. And that's when we found you."

I didn't know what to say. Why didn't he do what he was told and bring me down? (Guess he's not a good kid after all.)

Soon, we heard a loud chime go off. Mandel looked at his watch. "Man, it's getting late. Well, Carlos and I got a meeting to go to. We'll be back by nine. Alistair will be here if you need him."

He then got up from the chair he sat on and kissed my forehead. "Good night," he said as he left the room.

Good night? It was night already. I leaned over to look at the clock on my nightstand. Seven thirty in the evening it said; I was out of it that long.

I didn't know what to do. It wasn't like I could go and explore my new home. Soon there was a knock at the door. "Come in," I yelled. I waited to see who it was; but no one entered the room. I waited for another five minutes.

When no one came in, I thought that I would go and get into my PJs. After all, it's not like I would be going anywhere yet this evening. I pulled off the covers that were on me. I grabbed the crutches that were on the floor next to my bed. I hobbled over to the bathroom. There was a tank top and PJ pant with whale designs to put on. (Oh, different animals every night.)

I put on the clothes, combed my hair, and brushed my teeth. I unlocked the door and came out of the bathroom. Once I came out of the room, the lights went out; I screamed. No more than a second later, someone grabbed my neck. I wrapped my hands over the coarse fingers that obviously belonged to a man and tried to get him to let go of my fragile neck. My crutches dropped. Somehow, I got the man to let go. I screamed again and again.

Then he pushed me, and I fell down. I moved my hands, trying to find my crutches; but they were gone.

All of a sudden, the lights come on; Alistair was in the room. I looked around to see who the person was. Alistair had his little derringer out. He walked cautiously over to where I was laying on the floor.

He was only three feet away from me when all of a sudden, out of nowhere, M2 came up behind him. He had a dagger in his left hand.

What was I to do? I could not walk, and my leg hurt uncontrollably. "Alistair, look out," I yelled.

Alistair quickly spun around. At the same time, M2 swiped his dagger out across Alistair's chest.

All I could see was Alistair's hand reaching for his wound. Then at the same time, he fell to the ground. As I watched Alistair hit the ground, I knew that it was over. I was done for. But what did I do? I didn't know him (M2) until the plane here.

What did I ever do to him? Or was it what my parents did? He had every opportunity to kill them. Besides, he was evil enough.

Soon, I came back to reality. M2 came walking over to me with the dagger in front of him. In only a couple of minutes, I would be dead. And Alistair would have gotten hurt to help me.

Without any hope, I laid down, closing my eyes, waiting to die. M2 brought up his knife. In a couple seconds, it would be all over. The only thing that I could do was pray . . .

My parents never really went to church. They said that if God were real, then he wouldn't have them working with the Mafia. I never knew what to believe. I thought God was real. However, if he were, then why would he have me in this position? My friends told me about him, like how he healed the blind and made them see. Maybe he can heal me.

I opened my eyes to see if he was still there; he was. He was just about to drop it down on me when a loud bang went off. I didn't know what it was. I looked up at M2. He quickly sprang off and held his hand. It was covered in blood.

He looked over and glared at me. "I'll be back, don't you worry," he hissed as he left the room.

I looked over at Alistair. He had his derringer. I struggled to get up. I crawled helplessly over to get my crutches. Then I hopped over to the door. I opened it and yelled, "I need help in here!"

I couldn't stand in anymore. My leg hurt more than I could handle. I tried to walk back over to Alistair, but it was too much. I fell down and hit my head on a table stand. My head was now bleeding as well.

Soon, the door opened, and a maid (Linda) and a man (Max) came in. They both rushed over to me.

"Oh, miss," Linda said.

"I'll be fine, Alistair," I winced.

I watched them as they ran over to Alistair. Linda put his head on her lap. Then Max ripped open his shirt. It was soaked with blood. A big dark line went from one side of his chest to the middle.

Max then carefully picked him up and carried him over to the couch. "No, the bed, give him the bed," I told him.

Max obeyed and put him down on my bed. Then they came over and knelt down to me. "I'll get some bandages," Linda said.

Max put his hand up at my head. "What happened?" he asked.

My head was beating like a drum, but I managed to answer his question. "I came out from brushing my teeth when the lights went out. Someone grabbed my neck. Then he threw me on the floor. That was when Alistair came in. He put on the lights and saw me on the floor. He came over to me, and that was when the man came out again. I saw M2 came out with a dagger. I yelled for Alistair to watch out. He turned, and M2 swiped him in the chest. Then he came after me. But Alistair shot him in the hand," I explained.

I took a deep breath. Max nodded. Then Linda came in with some bandages. She gave Max a bandage to put on Alistair. Then she knelt down to put one on my head.

After I got my head wrapped up, she helped me to the couch. "Would you like some reading material until Sir Mandel gets back?" Linda asked me as she handed me a book.

The book was big and pink. The front cover said, "It's truly you," which was obviously the title. Then at the bottom, it said Maggie Renal. I had to laugh; what a stupid title. I mean, it clearly gives it away. The book is about romance. I have to deal with plenty of romance disasters in my life. I didn't have to read about it as well.

Even though I thought it was a stupid title, I thought I would give it a try. I flipped to the back to see what it was about.

> *Kelly just started a new year of school in ninth grade. And it just so happens that the boy of her dreams is in all of her classes. So she does not know any better than to go over and talk. However, that leads the boy, Kyle, to ask out Kelly. They are going out for a few weeks when Kelly thought it's Kyle whom she truly loves.*

I had to stop and read it three more times. It didn't make any sense. But it didn't matter for I wasn't going to read it anyway.

A groan of pain caught my attention. I looked over toward the bed for that was where the groan came from.

Alistair was holding his chest. Even though I was all the way at the couch, I could still see that he was sweating immensely. I didn't know what to do. I decided to try to get up to go and get him some help. But as I was trying to get up, the door opened, and in came Carlos and Mandel.

Mandel ran over to Alistair, and Carlos rushed over to me. "What has happened here?" he asked me with curiosity.

I laid back down for there was no reason for me to get up. "M2 came," I answered him.

He stared at me with surprising eyes. "M2 came? When did he come or how long after we left?"

I tried to concentrate but my brain wouldn't comprehend what Carlos was saying. It was as if my brain was having a malfunction; and it wouldn't collect everything that was needed to work correctly.

We heard another moan. Both Carlos and I looked over to see what was wrong. Even though we knew what was wrong already, Alistair was in agonizing pain. Okay, maybe I am stretching the truth just a little. But if you could have heard him, that is what you might think.

I tried to get up, but Carlos pushed me back down. He walked over to Mandel. "How bad do you think it is?" he asked.

Mandel sighed while getting up. "Well, the bleeding hasn't stopped. I can say one thing, M2 is lucky he didn't kill him. We'll have to call a doctor," Mandel said.

I looked over at him. "No, duh."

Mandel looked. "Excuse me!"

"Well, what about Natalie?" Carlos asked.

Mandel raised an eyebrow. "What about her?"

"Yeah, what about me?" I budded in.

Carlos sighed as if he wished he never asked. "Well, it's clear that M2 has a grudge on her. And it's clear that if it hadn't been for Alistair, M2 would have killed her. So she can't be alone. And with Alistair not being in any condition to move, where is she supposed to sleep?"

Mandel gave a little smirk. "Well, I know about all of those statements you made about M2, and as to where she is going to sleep, she is going to sleep with you. She can have the bed. As for you, you can have the couch. Since you are so cautious about her safety, you can be the one to look out for her. So you go call the doctor, and I'll stay with Alistair and Natalie," Mandel explained.

So as Mandel said, Carlos went out of the room to call for a doctor. But of course, these doctors are not like the ones that normal people have. Because of course, we are talking about the Mafia. Now they don't just bring in anyone. No, no. Whoever is involved has to go through many tests. And if it turns out that that person was going to give away the Mafia, "OFF WITH THEIR HEAD," as the king in the medieval times would say.

I stayed on the couch titling my thumbs while watching Mandel care for his son the best he could. "How bad do you think he is?" I asked with no warning.

Mandel looked up at him and sighed. "He's a tough kid. You should be very thankful. He will pull through this. He always does. It'll just take some time, that's all," Mandel answered.

As he finished up with what he was saying, Carlos came in with what do you know, a doctor. He was of average size, about five feet six inches. He had an eyeglass that laid on top of his flat nose. His eyes clearly gave away that he was Chinese. His suit was brown, an unusual color for a doctor. It was obviously expensive from the brand on the bottom of his coat—Sirikbom.

"Now, what seems to be the problem here?" the doctor asked.

"This is Dr. Hampton, Dad. I found him downstairs. He's supposed to check on Natalie, but I told him that Alistair was hurt bad," Carlos explained.

Dr. Hampton walked over to the bed. "Now, let's take off that bandage and get a look at the problem."

Mandel helped him take off the bandage. "My, what happened?"

"Someone was after Natalie, but Alistair stepped in," Mandel told the doctor.

"Well, I see. Um, there is not much I can do. He needs to stay in bed for at least a couple of days. I would normally say a week, but knowing you guys, you will probably get up two days later. But he must stay in at least two days. Then depending on how he feels, he can start to move. And always keep a clean bandage on him. And keep fluids in him," the doctor ordered Mandel. "But before I leave, I would like to look over at Natalie, if you don't mind."

"No, not at all," Mandel stated.

With a smile, he walked over toward me. "Well, Natalie, I hear that you hurt your leg," Dr. Hampton said with a grin.

I made a small smile. "A little bit. Nothing to be concerned about."

He took off the cast and squeezed my leg then he pressed in different spots. Soon, he pressed right on my ankle, and I winced in pain. "Aha, have you been resting it lately?"

"Well, it has been kind of busy . . ."

"That wasn't my question. Have you been resting it lately?" Dr. Hampton stopped me.

"No, sir. I have not been resting it."

He sighed as he got up from kneeling down. "Well, now you must listen to me. If you don't give that a couple of days to get back on the healing stage, you'll have to come into my office and have surgery on it. Do you understand, young lady?"

I nodded my head and laid back down on the couch. "Very well, I will check back with you in a couple of days."

Dr. Hampton took his black bag and then headed out of the room. After he left, Mandel looked at his watch. "Well, I think it is a perfect time to go to bed. Carlos, take Natalie and help her to your room so she can get some sleep. Then make your bed on the couch. I don't want to take any chances on M2 coming again," Mandel said.

Carlos sighed as I laughed. Then he came over, picked me up, and said, "Don't you think you're overreacting just a little?" he said as he took me to the door.

"Well, maybe just a little. But if I'm right, M2 has something against Natalie, and he won't stop until she's gone. But if anything did happen to her and I didn't take any caution, I wouldn't be able to forgive myself. Besides, you said yourself that it was dangerous. Now, go do as you're told," Mandel ordered.

I passed the halls as Carlos carried me with lack of struggle. "Carlos, am I heavy?" I asked him out of curiosity.

He thought it over for a while then answered, "If you were heavy, would I be able to do this?" he said as he threw me in the air and caught me again.

Then he gave me a soft smile. He gazed into my eyes. It was as if he was a ghost and was staring right through me. Only, his eyes were of kindness and love, not of hatred and evil. I stared back. I put my hands back around his neck to keep me from falling. Then as if it was natural and we were in a movie, our faces gradually made their way toward each other. Right when our lips were about to touch, I pulled my head back.

He looked away a second then focused forward again. "I'm sorry, please don't tell Alistair," Carlos pleaded.

I looked at him. "I am sorry, and I won't tell him if you don't," I apologized.

He nodded. "Those requirements are satisfactory." Soon, but not soon enough, we came to his room. He opened the door and turned on the light. He walked over and sat me down on the bed. "A maid will be in directly to bring in clothing for tomorrow."

I nodded as he left the room to go ask Mandel something. I felt so ashamed. I was just about to kiss my best friend/ future brother-in-law. I have somewhat betrayed Alistair. I backed up to pull down the covers.

Then I carefully crawled into bed. I closed my eyes, but nothing happened. I didn't go into la-la land like people say but stayed completely isolated from the rest of the earth. However, I didn't want to sleep but think about what might happen. What will happen tomorrow? Will Alistair be okay? When will I fill out those personnel files that Mandel talked about? Why did Carlos try to kiss me when he knew that I was Alistair's girlfriend? I probably could have picked plenty more questions, but they would just bore you to death.

CHAPTER 7

I guess I finally did go to sleep the night before because I woke to the sound of yelling. I sat up and looked to see if my crutches were put in here for me. Yes, they were. I struggled to get out of bed because my one foot was caught in the blankets.

Once I was free of the blanket, I had free access in which to get out of bed. Only for me, it was too much access. What I mean by too much access was that when I got away from the blanket, I fell. This was how I found out why the blanket was so hard to get off. All of the pressure was being taken on by that because the blanket was the only thing that was keeping me from falling. (I know it's confusing. Well, don't worry about that part, it's not important)

After my little clumsy incident, I *carefully* made my way to my crutches. After I felt safe again because I had my crutches, I made my way to the door. When I opened it, I heard another yell; it was Alistair.

I hurried as fast as I could down to my room. Well, not my room, but well, I hurried to go see what was going on. As soon as I came to the door, I heard another yell.

I opened the door to see Alistair sitting up in bed, yelling. "What is going on?" I asked as I walked in and closed the door behind me.

"I have to clean the wound, but in order to do that, I have to put on this disinfectant stuff on. And as you can see, it stings," Mandel explained.

"Well, at least he is awake," Carlos put in.

I looked over at him, still shocked about the other night. I will never think of him the same way again. After an incident like that, it would be hard. Even for you. However, he is still my friend, and for that, I must talk to him. I walked over to him and said, "Did you sleep well last night?"

He looked away and answered, "No. I was here the whole night."

Mandel looked at us as if he knew that there was something going on. I walked up to Alistair. "You're going to be okay," I said, trying to convince myself more than him.

He smiled while wincing from the pain. "That's enough, I got the disinfectant on. You can rest now," Mandal said.

Alistair smiled. "I'll be just fine. Hey, how is your leg doing?" he asked.

"Oh, fine."

Mandel smiled. "Well, everyone out. He needs to get some rest."

I nodded. And walked out of the room. Now what do I do? I headed for my room. Once I got to the arched door, I went inside. I looked around to see what was there to do. In addition, nothing. There was nothing to do in my bedroom. I mean, it was a lovely room with two big couches, a big bed, two huge windows facing the front of the house. A flat-screen TV, a desk with a laptop. There was everything, but all the things that were in my room were things that I didn't feel like using.

I didn't do anything for the rest of the day. Just stayed in bed then went to bed at night. However, on the following evening, I started to take a tour of my room. I touched the wall and the curtains as if I were in an open house. Soon, I came to a big bin. I looked inside—basketball, tennis racket with a ball. I couldn't play tennis. You need two people, and I wasn't about to ask Carlos to play. But you can play basketball with just one player.

I grabbed the basketball, grabbed my shows, and ran out of the room. I galloped down the stairs, making sure that I landed just right for my leg wasn't fully healed. (I know that you might think—that this book is "jacked up" because normally, a person wouldn't be able to do that. But my leg was really doing well. I guess I just sprained it.)

I walked outside and to the back of the house. It was dark, but I did not care for the yard light was on. I sped through the grass, anxious to get to the court and see how good I was.

I dropped the ball on the black top and started to dribble it up and down the court. As soon as I got the feel of it, I went up for a shot. It turned out that I was not that good. I dribbled back down the other side of the court and headed up for a right layup; I missed.

What I did know was that I was not so good. What I did not know was that Yassen, one of my friends and second-in-command of the Mafia, was watching me from a distance. I only found out about this when I heard, "Did you play?"

Startled, I turned around. Once I knew that it was only Yassen, I let out a deep breath. "Oh, Yassen, sir, um, you nearly gave me a heart attack," I sighed.

He came out of the shadows. "I am sorry. Do forgive me. Like I was saying earlier, did you play?"

I slapped the ball down hard onto the black top and then answered, "I used to. Like when I was ten or eleven. Why do you ask me?"

He shrugged as he took the ball and dribbled it up to do a left layup. It was smooth and, like, so cool. The net actually made a swoosh noise when the ball came through the net.

All I did was stare as he made his way back to me. "Wow. I didn't know you could play."

He looked away at the house. "You never asked. Mandel is watching us. I bet you didn't know he could play."

My eyes grew big. "I didn't think the Mafia knew how to be normal. Well, I don't mean *normal . . .*"

I did not finish because I did not know what to say. "It's okay. I know what you mean. However, believe it or not, we were young once too," Yassen said while grinning

We went to sit down on a bench when we saw Mandel make his way outside. "Well, what might you two be doing?" he asked.

"Oh, just telling her what we used to do when we were little," Yassen explained to him.

"I didn't know you played basketball," I said with my eyes wide with curiosity.

"Ah," Mandel said as he put his hands on his knees to ease down next to me on the bench. "You never asked me."

I sighed. "Is that all you people say around here? Do you think you could still play?"

"Um, I don't know. Why? Or don't I want to know?"

"Well, I thought that you and Yassen could play a game."

Both of them looked at me. "You what?" Mandel asked me.

"Oh, come on, Mandel, you're not that old, are you? Come on, I'm kind of curious what kind of shape I'm in," Yassen said, smiling, as he got up and took the ball from me.

"Well, all right. Only one game."

"Deal."

I knew from the time that Yassen got up that this was going to be entertaining. I watched them line up at the circle. Yassen had a serious face on as if he was getting ready to fight someone who cheated money off him in a poker game. On the other hand, Mandel was cracking up, laughing, almost making Yassen brake his emotionless face.

Then they were off. Yassen dribbled the ball down the left side of the court. Then with no warning, Mandel came, stole the ball, and headed back in the other direction.

My eyes were wide; they were acting as if they were kids again. They were yelling at each other when one of them took the ball away from each other and gave each other high fives when one of the made a basket.

Soon, the game was over. They came over, waiting to hear who won. I was calculating who made the most baskets. "So who won? Me?" Yassen said while pointing to himself and smiling. "Or him?" and pointed to Mandel. Mandel laughed and elbowed him in the shoulder.

I sighed. "Well, Yassen, I hate to tell you this, but you need to work on your blocking. Twenty-eight to twelve. Mandel wins!"

Yassen gave Mandel a high five and said, "Good job, man."

"Thanks. Well, it is time for supper. Natalie, why don't you go get changed and let me and Yassen talk."

"Okay," I agreed. I said good-bye.

I turned as started to walk into the house.

Mandel turned to Yassen. "She's getting the hang of this lifestyle," Mandel said. The both of them watched her walk into the house.

"Yes, she is," Yassen said.

At supper, we had lamb and potatoes. They were good. The table was quiet with only Yassen, Carlos, Mandel, and me. However, after I was done eating, I took up Alistair's food.

I knocked on the door to be polite and went in. Alistair was reading a magazine. He went in and saw me. "Oh, hi."

I smiled as I came in with the tray. "I thought you would be hungry," I said.

He motioned for me to sit while he put the magazine away. I gave him the tray, and he gave me a kiss on the cheek.

He ate his lamb and potatoes as he talked to me about different things. "So really, how's your leg?" he asked me.

I looked at my leg, as if waiting for it to tell me itself. "Um, okay. I can still feel it. But I was playing basketball so I guess it's going good. How about you?"

"Honestly, I feel like and I bet I look like a sick mull."

I gave a little chuckle. "Well, hey, at least you can start walking around tomorrow."

He gave a little laugh. "Can you keep a secret?"

I nodded. "Well, I always had this sort of what you could call *gift* that I heal faster than others, and well, I have been walking since, well, a little bit before you came in."

I was stunned. He was stabbed in the chest, and only a couple of days afterward, he is walking. "Okay, that's just a little, um, yeah, okay. Oh, um, Alistair, I didn't get a chance to say this yet, but thanks for what you did that night. I mean, if it was not for you, I would have been dead. And I sort of feel responsible for you getting hurt."

He shook his head. "Oh, come on. That is nonsense. I chose to help you. And I made the right choice."

I smiled but looked down. "Hey, I got something for you. It is in your room. I ordered it for you. Go and tell me what you think."

I looked up, all happy now. "Okay."

I ran all the way to my room. When I got to my door, I pushed it open and looked for it.

There it was on my bed. A Shih Tzu, a doggy. I went over to pet it. It had a collar on that said Snickers. Then over next to my bed was a small pillow for it and a whole bunch of other things like treats, toys, and other things. I looked for a leash and put it on her. I walked her over to Alistair's room. Once I was in, I gave him a big smile and ran to give him a hug.

"Thanks."

"You're welcome," he said.

I stayed there for the rest of the night, well, until I went to bed of course.

Do not get any ideas.

CHAPTER 8

"She has been here for almost a month, and it has been fine!"

"That may be, but we don't know what she might do in the future," Yassen Bicker said.

Mandel sighed, "Yassen, you are like the closest friend I had since I started with you. But what I can't understand is why you would do something like this to me."

Yassen sighed as Mandel did. "I know."

"Then why are you doing this?" argued Mandal.

"I am just being cautious."

"There is no need to be, she is fine. And just remember that I am the head of the Mafia, and to me, you're just a shrimp so be careful on what you say."

"Fine, sir, but just remember, I'm not the only one who wants her out."

Mandel leaned forward in his chair. "If you so lay a finger on her, I will make sure that you're the one who gets thrown out and not her. And I hope you know what we do to people so they don't talk."

Yassen nodded.

I was walking in the halls after I finished lunch in the kitchen. I always loved the smell of the freshly baked bread in the oven. I was walking in the west wing when I heard yelling coming from the door. I looked to see what was on the door sign, CONFERENCE ROOM 1. I thought that I should maybe back away, but as I was doing so, I heard my name. So naturally, I put my ear up to the door, but soon after, I wish I did not.

"Why don't you believe me that she will not say anything?" Mandel questioned.

Yassen completely avoided the question but stated, "There is no choice; Natalie must die!"

"Yassen, I know you love her as I do. Please tell me what is going on."

He shook his head. "No, I can't."

"Please."

"Fine, in my room at three o'clock."

Mandel nodded.

I think you can guess that that was when I wished that I did not stop to listen in. I was in tears; they wanted to kill me. I turned and ran to my room.

As soon as I got back to my room, I grabbed a bag. I walked over to my closet and pulled out two shirts, jeans, and a jacket. Then I went over to my nightstand and pulled out a hundred and fifty bucks. I looked over at Snickers and remembered how I promised I was going to take her on a walk later; well, I couldn't take her along. I gave her a hug and turned off the light as I closed the door again.

I ran downstairs. When I was running for the door, I bumped into one of my maids, Prinella. "Miss, are you going somewhere?" she asked.

I did not want to answer but just, like, go away. "Um, tell Mandel that I went away for a while," I answered her.

I do not think she understood what I was doing by running away. Nevertheless, I was glad. I did not want anything to get in my way.

After I answered her, I ran off. I did not look back, but I think I almost saw her try to grab my shirt to stop me. I ran out the door and stopped once more when I got to the end of the driveway. I looked back once more; I thought I was like part of their family. We did everything together. I even became good friends with one of the cooks, Cubochie.

I started walking; but the more I walked, I just felt that someone was following me so I started to run. I ran all the way into town. The stone street made me feel like in the ancient times when people like me ran away and ran into a town like this, trying to escape death. I did not know why it took stone streets to make me realize that, but well, it did.

I soon came to a nice easy walk. I guess because I thought that if they did try to chase me, there were enough people in this town for me to blend in. As I walked through the streets, everyone made way for me. They smiled and waved as I smiled as well.

Mandel made his way up to Yassen's room. He looked at his watch—three o'clock. Once he got there, he gave a knock and helped himself in. He found Yassen standing there at the window. "You said you were going to tell me what was going on," Mandel reminded.

"So I have," Yassen said. "Please have a seat," he pointed at the table and chairs without looking.

Mandel took his seat as Yassen has offered. "Now, why do you want Natalie dead?" Mandel started.

"I don't want her dead," Yassen said, almost sounding stressed. "M2 came to me a couple of days ago and said that if I don't convince you to kill her, then I will be his target instead of Natalie. Now that I think of it, Natalie is too precious. And I don't care if I die, but she won't."

Mandel nodded. "Thank you for telling me. Now how about we go downstairs and play a game of pool. I bet I'll beat you."

Yassen laughed but agreed.

As they made their way downstairs, Prinella ran up to them and gasped, "Sir, I am sorry I didn't say anything earlier, but I thought she only went for a walk. Miss Natalie has been gone for a couple of hours."

Mandel looked at his watch. "Where do you think she went?" Yassen asked.

"I don't know. Go get Carlos, and we will look around. Thank you, Prinella."

And with that, both of them went off. (Forget about the pool game. They're playing an old-fashioned game of treasure hunt.)

Soon, unbelievingly, I was getting tired. I didn't want to go back, but I didn't think that the *Mafian princess* should really sleep on the cold stones of the street. Even though there probably won't be a Mafian princess anymore after tomorrow. That is if they were in a hurry to kill me. But why? Well, anyway, soon, it was five in the evening. I didn't understand how it could be that late already, but when you observe what has happened and how long it took, you get some questions answered. (What I mean is that when I was snooping and listening in on their conversation about killing me, I had just been done with lunch. And it took me ten minutes to pack and about an hour and a half to get into town. Then I was walking around for about two hours so I guess it's possible, especially if I had lunch at two.)

I kept walking around, trying to think about what I was going to do for the night. Like, where I was going to sleep and what I was going to do for breakfast in the morning. When I was just about to turn off to go onto the country road, I heard, "Natalie!"

I tensed up, wondering if I should run or not. Then I heard it again, and it was a girl's voice. I turned around to see Vashti, one of my good friends, running toward me. "Where are you going?" Vashti asked me.

"Away," I answered her with an emotionless expression.

"What? Why? It's almost dark."

I looked back to my original destination—the country (a.k.a. wildness) Then I started to have tears in my eyes.

Vashti gave one look at me and knew something was wrong. "What is it?"

I looked at her. "I'm scared."

She came around and put her arm around my shoulders. "Come, let's go to my house, and we can have a cup of tea and talk."

Hesitantly, I followed her. Vashti was only seventeen and already owned a house. But she still acted like a child (but you didn't need to know that).

I followed her to her mud brick house. It wasn't big but not small either. She opened the door, and we went in. She had me sit down. She went into the kitchen as I dried my childish tears. Soon she came out to give me a cup of tea.

She sat down and put her hand on my knee. "Natalie, what's wrong?"

I took the cup up to my lips and take a sip. "Yassen is trying to get Mandel to kill me."

Once Vashti heard this, her tea came rushing out of her mouth like a waterfall out of a cave. (In other words, she spitted out her tea.)

"You're kidding me. Why? I thought Yassen loved you."

"Me too. I mean, he did everything for me. He even got me out of doing work when I wanted to do shopping. So why would he want me dead?"

Vashti looked at me and gave me an eye. "Do you think someone put him up to it?"

I shook my head even though I knew that if anyone would, then it would probably be M2.

When Vashti realized I was lying, she gave me an eye again. Only it wasn't like the one before. I would say it was like the kind you mother would give you if you said you didn't really eat all of the cookies in the cookie jar. "Natalie Maclusta, now you tell me the truth. Do you know anyone who would want to bribe Yassen to trying to kill you?"

I decided to tell the truth because I know that she would do anything to get her way. "Fine, well this one guy, M2 . . ."

I stopped from the sound that Vashti made. "Is something wrong?" I asked her.

She shook her head and said, "Nothing, it's just that a couple of days ago, M2 rode into town. He was furious because no one, like, bowed down to him. He said that he was going to get his job back and that then we'll be sorry. Along with other things that he did that were the norm."

I nodded understandingly. I looked at my wrist as if I had a watch and got up. "Yeah, well, I better get going."

She stood up right after I did. "So where are you going? Home or are you still insisting on going away?"

I stood and thought for no more than a minute when we heard yelling outside. Both Vashti and I ran to the door and opened it just a crack. "Natalie Maclusta! Just because Mandel chose not to kill you doesn't mean I won't. So just remember that you can run, but you can't hide. And just so you know, I wasn't about to give up because I couldn't get you that one night because your little boyfriend helped you," yelled a man.

I put my head down and then quickly ran over to get my things. "Do you have a back door?" I asked Vashti.

She gave me a sympathetic smile and had me follow her to the back of the house. "If you need anything, you know where to find me," she said.

I smiled as I went to give her a hug. "I know." Then I turned and went out the door.

I walked out and saw a little stone path to get out onto the street. I followed it but stayed close to the wall of the house. As soon as I got to the road, I saw him, M2. He was on a horse. (For some reason, he reminds me of a prince in the midevil times. This whole place reminds of the midevil times.)

Only he wasn't a very good prince. More like the ones who act nice until he gets what he wants then the true him comes out. And let me tell you, you better watch out.

I watched a little longer before I planned my move. I decided to run as fast as I could and hope for the best. I sprinted out. Unfortunately, he noticed me even before I got across the road. He made his big muscular legs kick the horse's side, and he was off. I could hear him gallop up after me. I wanted to look back but was too scared that if I did, it would only make him go faster.

I felt everyone's eye on me. "Would she make it, or would she crash and burn?" was probably what they were thinking as they watched. I felt as if I was walking on air but then I found out that the only reason for that was that M2 had his hand on the collar of my shirt. I wanted to scream.

I heard everyone gasp as M2 came to a stop. He didn't let go but managed to get down without loosening his grip on my neck. He dragged me into a small house nearby. I wondered what we were going to do in there, but I managed to keep my curiosity under control.

I followed him in without any trouble. He shoved me over to a sofa. He marched over to me and pulled me up by my shirt. "What am I going to do with you?" he hissed at me. His smelled of fresh cologne, and his shirt was freshly washed.

I looked up at him with emotionless eyes. I wasn't about to let him think that I was scared, even though I was. I grinned at him. "Well, we can do a replay in old movies. I ask for you to let me go, but I think you are too smart for that," I replied to his first statement.

"Don't sass me. Or you will be one dead puppy."

"I wasn't sassing you. But I could if you want me to."

"You are nothing but a little wretch. You know that."

I smiled. "Yeah, I know. However, it takes one to know one."

He glared at me as I did to him. "I don't like you."

"Goes both ways." I managed to keep talking. "You don't like me, and I don't like you." I started to move slowly. I started to stand up. Unbelievably, he started to let go of his grip. Finally, I was loose. "I know why I don't like you, but I don't know why you don't like me. You have been trying to kill me since I came here. I barely even know you."

"That's funny because I know a lot about you. And as to why I don't like you, well, you'll just have to find out. But wait, too bad, you won't get the chance."

Then no later than a second, he pulled out a blade. "Because you'll be to dead to even think about what happened."

I started to show that I was scared. I was backing up. I started to make little panicky noises.

He started to walk toward me. I looked right and left; there was nowhere to run. I was going to die in less than five minutes. (But that's what I thought that last time too.)

I looked at him straight in his eye. Trying to mentally reason with him. His eyes were like a swamp—no feelings. Doesn't matter how hard you try to reason with it, you just keep on sinking to your death.

He looked at me with his cold, icy eyes that seemed to pierce right through me; I shivered.

He was soon only about one foot away from me when the door slammed open. In walked Carlos and Mandel (the good one).

M2 turned around, stunned to see his twin brother there. "What do you want?" he spat at him.

"You either put down that knife or I will do it for you," Mandel said.

Carlos walked slowly yet carefully over to where I was. "Natalie, come," he whispered.

Mandel dropped the cape he was wearing on the chair next to him. "You will leave Natalie alone from now on. Do you understand?"

Carlos took my hand and walked over behind Mandel. I pulled my hand away, not looking at him.

M2 looked at Mandel with cold, harsh eyes. (Yes, I know, it's confusing. Just focus, and you'll get it.) "Why did you do this? You knew that I would get revenge. So when you think about it, this is all your fault," M2 said.

"You knew that this was coming someday, and you chose to have it end like this. I said that you could have a different position, but you wouldn't listen to reason."

M2 looked at me. "I don't care, but the next time I see that young lady, she will die."

Mandel stepped forward two steps. "Well, then, you will have to kill me first."

He started to walk away when M2 pulled up his knife and started to move forward. Carlos and I watched with concerned eyes. A couple of weeks ago, Mandel told me that he was trained by the CIA. I would have never believed him without the proof of this moment.

M2 was no more than a couple of inches from slashing that knife into Mandel's back when he spun around and did a round-house kick and knocked the knife right out of his hands. Then he did an axe kick right up M2's face. He staggered back. "Now stay away," Mandel repeated as he walked away.

He placed his hand on my back and motioned me to walk forward. Once we were out of the house, the townspeople were still there, watching what was happening. I saw his limo a little ways down the road.

I saw Vashti on the side of the road, and she ran toward me. "Are you all right?" she asked me.

I looked at Mandal and Carlos, "Yeah, just fine."

Mandel and Carlos kept walking while Vashti and I kept talking. Soon enough, Mandel didn't look back but yelled, "Natalie, it's time to go!"

He spoke with a tone I never heard him speak in. We gave each other a quick hug, and I hurried off.

Carlos got in first and then Mandel motioned for me to get in the middle. The limo driver closed the door once Mandel got in.

There was silence in the car. I looked at both Mandel and Carlos. Neither one of them looked back at me and smiled. "I'm sorry," I said finally, feeling like a little kid again.

Like before, Mandel didn't look at me but said, "You should be."

"I am. But you don't have to be so rude."

Mandel made a sarcastic laugh. "Rude? You have everything you want. You normally don't have to do anything that you don't want to do. Why would you run? Especially when you know that my brother wants and is trying to kill you. If your maid didn't mention something to me that you just got up and left, you would be dead right now. You will never do this again!"

I looked down, almost feeling ashamed. "*Sorry*, but I was walking down the hallway after lunch, and I heard someone talking about me in Conference Room 1. So I was really quiet so I could hear. I knew I shouldn't have, but I did, and Yassen was trying to get you to kill me. What was I supposed to do? Just walk away and pretend like I never heard that?"

Mandel nodded. "You are correct about all that, but we weren't going to kill you. I would never allow that, you should know that. It turned out that my brother has threatened to kill Yassen if he didn't talk to me about it. That is all."

I opened my mouth to say something when Mandel butted in, "We'll talk about this when we get home!"

I never heard him yell. Well, not at me anyway. I think that was my cue to be quiet.

It was silent for the rest of the drive. Once we got home, I got out and headed for the door. I was about to go in when Mandel called my name. "Natalie! I would like to have a word with you in your room in ten minutes."

I nodded and headed up to my room. I was going to get it. Even though I was going out with his son, he really felt like a dad to me. I mean, I loved my parents even though I didn't think of them much since they died. I guess to save the pain. But my father never punished me. I never thought that I would feel closer to a man who is the head of the Mafia and who is in no relation with me than my own parents.

I made my way to my room, exiting from my thoughts. I opened the door to my room and got on clean clothes and put the dirty ones in the laundry basket. I went over and laid on my bed until I heard a knock on my door. "You may enter," I said, already knowing who it was—Mandel.

He gave a weak smile as he came in and closed the door. He walked over and sat down on the bed next to me. "I think we need to talk."

I nodded. "I think so too."

"Now, you ran away, you didn't tell anyone. Don't you think that that deserves some punishment?"

I shrugged my shoulders. "I guess, but two days?"

Mandel rolled his eyes. "Natalie, you are being like a little girl. Two days is not long at all. I know that I am not you father, but before he died and we were working together, he made me promise that if anything ever did happen to them, you would be my responsibility. And when you ran away, I remembered that. I was worried about you, Natalie. Just because I'm not your father doesn't mean I can't worry about you. And I know that this might hurt, but I will be like a father to you and so you will be grounded for two days. This is one that you will not get out of."

I nodded. "Okay. I guess two days isn't that bad. But seriously, I am, like, fifteen. I think I am a little old to be grounded."

Mandel gave a little laugh. "Girl, you're lucky my parents weren't yours. I was spanked until I was fifteen. So I think you might as well take the grounding."

I gave him a little smile to make sure that he knew that I was joking. He made a little chuckle and patted my leg. As soon as he got up, the door slammed open. It was Alistair. He didn't seem very happy. "Hi," I said.

Mandel laughed as walked out the door. Alistair closed the door. "You are in big trouble, young lady," he said.

I rolled my eyes. I thought that Mandel was acting like my dad, but Alistair was the best. He put his hand up to his chest. (His chest still must hurt.)

I nodded. "Yep, I'm grounded for two days."

He gave a look that stated that I was pathetic. "That's all? Two days? When I ran away two years ago, I was, like, grounded for a month. It's probably because you're not his biological daughter. But how stupid are you to run away? You didn't even tell me."

I looked down. "Well, you would have stopped me. And in future reference, I thought you don't normally tell people when you run away. That sort of ruins the whole point."

At first, he looked at me like, *Where did that come from?* then he started to walk over to me. "No, I would have come with you. But I guess I'm not important enough."

He turned and started to walk out. "Wait," I called, but there was no use. He didn't stop to listen to what I had to say or pause and think twice about what he was doing. He walked out of the door and slammed it behind him.

Now, to sum things up for you, if you got stuck or confused about anything. I'll help you. I got scared thinking Mandel was going to kill me and ran away, but it didn't work because Mandel #2 found me and was about to kill me if it wasn't for Mandel's wonderful timing. And so he saved me and grounded me for two days. And now for some strange, awkward reason, Alistair's mad at me.

CHAPTER 9

I stared at the door that Alistair just walked out of. What did I do? I didn't think that he would want to go with me. He didn't have to yell at me. I got up from sitting on my bed and walked over to my window. I looked out. Two men were there, talking to Alistair. Then soon, a horse came, and the three of them left.

I watched as they faded away into the evening's light. Where were they going? was a question that I had and knew that would never be answered. An expression of puzzlement crossed my face. Who were the two gentlemen whom my boyfriend just ride away with? I was tempted to follow them, but I didn't feel like it. Not for now anyway. I was startled by a knock that came from the door.

I turned around while answering, "Come in."

The door slowly opened. Carlos closed the door behind him. I looked at him and turned to face the window again. "I know that you probably don't want to talk to me, but we need to get something straight," he concluded.

I didn't turn to face him but stated, "What?"

"The night that I was taking you in my room and we almost kissed, that was a mistake. That should not have been done. I know that we will never forget that, but we can't let it come between us. I fear that since then, you have been avoiding me. Natalie, I have been your best friend since, well, forever. We did everything together. Please don't end it with a little mistake."

With the end of his sentence, he turned to walk out the door and closed it with a bang.

I thought about what he said. I know that what I did was wrong, almost kissing him; but like he said, it was a mistake. And I shouldn't let that come between us. I smiled to myself and ran for the in a hurry to see if I could catch up with him. I opened the door and looked left and right. I saw him heading for the stairs.

"Carlos," I called.

I saw him look back. "Do you want to play some tennis?" I saw him smile. "Okay, I'll see you in the court in fifteen minutes," he yelled.

I smiled back at him as I headed back into my room to get changed.

Once I was outside, I looked up at the sky. It was cool yet warm. I looked at my wrist for it showed the time. Six in the evening. It was a little late to be playing tennis, but I didn't mind.

I made my way to the back of the house for that was where the tennis court was. To my surprise, Carlos was already there.

I walked onto the court, ready to play. Carlos threw the first ball.

My eyes focused on the ball as I ran to the left. I them swat back at it, making it bounce three times before hitting Carlos's racket. It flew back at me.

After playing it for about an hour, we sat down to talk. "Where did Alistair go?" was the first thing that came out of my mouth.

Carlos looked away while throwing a piece of grass to the side. "Every week, a few other guys and he go and ride around town and out of town to see if there is any mischief going on. Basically, he is the police around. Only, well, never mind, all he does is ride around and see what's going on. That's all," he explained.

I nodded. "I think he is mad at me."

"Well, we were all worried about you. You should have seen him. He was pacing back and forth right outside the door in case you came back."

I looked down at my knees, now ashamed. "Sorry I ran away. It's just that I was scared and I had to get away from it."

He nodded in agreement. "I see. Well, Alistair should be back by about . . . What time is it now?"

"Eight thirty."

"Oh, wow, it's late. Um, well, he should be back by eleven. Well, I am going to go in and get a snack. Wanna come along?"

"No. I think I might take a ride up at the trail. I didn't get to see that yet."

He shrugged. "Whatever. I'll put on the lamp for you so you don't get lost."

"Okay, thanks. Oh, and Carlos?"

Carlos stopped walked turned around and said, "Yeah?"

"I'm sorry for being a brat and not being very nice."

"Well, you always were a brat," he said while laughing.

"That's not funny," I said to him, laughing as well. Then *playfully*, I threw my tennis racket at him. "Take this in."

Then he went inside while I walked to the stables. I opened the big wooden door and head to got saddle up my horse, Midnight. She was born wild. (Yeah, you didn't really need to know that.)

I headed to the tack room. I didn't know which one to get for the one that I used before wasn't there. However, I decided for the one next to it. I carried it back to the stable and saddled her.

Finally, I was ready to go out. I got on Midnight and started off on a canter then on a run. As soon as I found the trail, I slowed to a trot. I decided to make her walk in case anything happened. (Don't ask me what would happen because I don't have a clue.)

I was walking for a while, like, I don't know how long I was riding, but it seemed to be like for, um, maybe, like, a couple of hours.

Soon I heard a noise. The horse started to neigh. I tried to pull back the reins to keep it from making too much noise. Then there was rustling in the trees. I squinted my eyes to try to see it, but it was too dark. It got louder and louder. Then I saw it. You won't believe this, but it was a rabbit.

I swiped my forehead as if relieved. After all the ruckus, I continued on my walk. I was looking around surprised how bright it was with the oil lamps that were on. (Well, they weren't oil, but they looked like them, and they were electric. Well, I think.)

Everything was nice and calm after that until I heard a noise again. I didn't really do anything, thinking that it was another rabbit. But that was when I realized that rabbits don't exactly have hooves to make *tapping* sounds on the black top. I looked behind me and started to gallop, and that turned into a hard, fast run.

I always wondered past the trail. I'm not going to say that I was glad that someone was behind me. But if someone wasn't, then I probably would never find out. I ran for about a couple more minutes when I looked in front of me. The trail just sort of ended.

I was now out in the middle of nowhere. I looked around me. It looked like I was in a big field. It was beautiful.

I could still hear the person behind me. I kicked Midnight to make her run. I'll have to enjoy the scenery some other time. I ran across the plain. I heard someone shouting behind, but I didn't care to look. That was until I heard my name.

I stopped and looked behind me. He was too far away from me. Then he came into focus; it was Alistair.

I was going to kill him. He always knew how to scare me, but this tops everything. I started to run his way. "What the hell do you think we're doing?" I said as soon as I knew he could hear me.

"I came home earlier than I expected, and Carlos said that you were taking the trail, and I thought that I would come up and surprise you."

I rolled my eyes. "I thought you were mad at me?"

"Yeah, well, I gave it a lot of thought and came to the conclusion that if I was in the same situation, then I probably would have done the same thing. So in conclusion, I'm sorry."

I didn't expect for him to say that so I didn't know what to say. "Um, well, oh. That's okay."

He smiled and started to trot in the direction that I was running a few minutes ago. "Now, where are you going?"

"To do sightseeing. Wanna come along?"

I squinted my eyebrows together in confusion then smiled and starting riding in his direction.

We rode down the big field. He would come and push my horse with his, and we would laugh, and I would chase him around.

We stayed out there for what would be most of the night. I don't remember going to bed until after three.

Chapter 10

Mandel was up at six, thinking in his room in his chair. Carlos, Alistair, *and* Natalie never had to go through what he did when he was little. So he thought that what they needed was a little discipline.

He walked out of his room and headed for Natalie's room. He opened the door and saw Snickers lying on her bed next to her. "Natalie," he yelled.

When she didn't wake up, he went over put Snickers on the floor and pulled the covers off the bed.

I woke up to see Mandel standing in front of me. I then noticed that all of my covers were on the floor in a big pile. "What happened?" I asked, half-asleep.

Mandel smiled. "Time to get up," he said.

"You have got to be kidding me."

"Nope, time to get to work."

After he said that, he started to leave the room. "What work?" I asked, scared.

He didn't answer me until he was just about to close the door. "Yep, boot camp. Get dressed."

My mouth dropped open as I heard him laughing down the hallway. He thought this was funny.

Even though I didn't want to, I got out of bed and got dressed. I was a little curious to see if he was joking or not.

When I got downstairs, I saw Alistair and Carlos standing there, dressed. Alistair was half-awake like I was, but Carlos was fully awake. "Now, I have been thinking about when I was young like you. I wasn't as easy. And so you three are going to boot camp," Mandel explained.

"What?" we said all at the same time.

"Yep, I set up a course of what you would like to call mini-boot camp. Yassen is going to be the one in charge. It'll be one week.

And then I will see if we will have to go any further with this. I guess you can call it an experiment. You will wear uniforms."

"Okay, one week," I said, thinking that I was losing my mind for going along with this.

"Yep."

"Okay, I'll do it."

"Um, Natalie?"

"Yeah?"

"I don't think you get it. Even if you didn't want to do it, you would have to anyway. But thank you for saying that you would do it."

The boys laughed at me and I gave them an eye. "You will start tomorrow. You can go now."

After he left, I looked at the guys and smiled. "I am going to kill you!"

I wasn't really going to do anything to them but chase them. I think they knew that because they laughed and started to run away.

I chased them outside. Finally, they were cornered by the stable door. I then finally reached up to them, obviously not as fast as them. We all laughed then. "Now what?" I said, still panting.

"Oh, I don't know. Do you want to watch TV?" Carlos asked.

Alistair and I looked at each other. "Okay," we both said at the same time.

"As long as it's your room. Mandel said that when we watch TV, he can hear it all the way from the east wing so we can't watch it downstairs," I said.

"Not my room," Carlos complained.

I looked at Alistair, hoping he would say that we could do it in his room. (Don't get any ideas.)

"Nope" was Alistair's answer.

They both then looked at me. "Fine," I said, knowing that didn't have any chance arguing against two other boys.

We walked up to my room. I ran out in front to open it before they got there. When I opened it, my room was a mess. I screamed, thinking that was the appropriate thing to do. Alistair and Carlos came running to see what happened. Alistair pulled out his derringer and pushed me aside. He walked in and then looked back at me. I knew that look, it was bad.

He walked around the room but stopped and looked down and put his derringer back in his shirt.

"What? What is it," I asked half-scared.

When he didn't answer, I pushed past Carlos and hurried to Alistair's side. Once I spotted what Alistair was looking at, I screamed. There laid Snickers. Dead as could be. It looked like a rated-M video. Blood was all over him. I was building up vengeance inside me. Who could do a thing like this? I started to think of people even though I already knew who did it—M2.

Alistair got up from where he was kneeling, patted my shoulder, and walked over to the table next to my bed. At first, I didn't know what he was doing, but when I actually looked over at the table, I noticed a little card and a little box. The card said,

> *Miss Natalie,*
>   *I think you should clean up you room. It's a mess. Hope you understand the act of war. And don't forget the next time that I try to kill you, I will succeed.*
>
>   *-M2*

Alistair got done reading the card and gave it to me. I felt a hand come up and touch my shoulder. I gave a little gasp but heard, "It's okay, it's only me." I looked behind me; it was only Carlos. I gave him a weak smile.

Alistair opened the box, but when he did, "Alistair, I am imagining that you are there right now with Natalie listening to this as well as Carlos. So I am just going to say this now. I am close. And the next time that I want to kill Natalie, you will not be around to hear her screams or to save her. And the Miss Natalie, I am sorry that all this had to happen but when you think about it, it's all your fault. So deal with it" came out. It was M2's voice.

I breathed in deeply, trying to concentrate. How was this my fault? Before any of the boys could say anything, the door opened, and in walked Mandel. His eyes widened as he looked around the room. And when he saw poor little Snickers there, lying, he looked at me. "Are you all right?" he asked.

"Yes, I am," I replied.

"Now who is going to tell me what happened?"

Alistair looked at his father. "Your brother is playing games on us."

Mandel nodded. "He seems to like doing that."

"May I ask a question," I asked while raising my hand as if I was in school again.

Mandel nodded. "Oh course. What is it?"

"Um, in the disturbing message M2 sent me he said that for me not to blame him for what has happened but to blame myself. What have I done for him to say that. Again if I may ask."

"Aye. Natalie, I am so sorry. I never told you. I never even though. Sit down and I will tell you."

I looked over at the bed and the sofa then looked back at Mandel with an *Are you serious.?* Face. "Well, I guess not here. Come into my study and I will tell you there. I started to follow him when he looked back at Alistair and Carlos standing there. "You may come to."

Alistair nodded. "I want to call the maids first."

All of us nodded. When we opened the door, the maid surprised us by already being there.

"Ah, you are good, now I want you to clean up Miss Natalie's room," Alistair ordered.

The maids bowed. "Yes, sir, we will deal with that decisively," one maid said.

We then decided to wait for Alistair. We all walked down the hall together then. Mandel opened the door for me and motioned to me to go into the room. He closed the door as soon as all of us were in. I went and sat down on one of the chairs.

"Now," Mandel started to say as he sat down, "long ago when your parents started to work for me, my brother was second-in-command. Within a couple of weeks, they were higher in command that Yassen. And then soon they got good enough to even be better than M2. I had to think about it a lot but came to the conclusion to not let someone like your parents leave. I told M2 that he was going to be knocked down and that your parents were going to take his place. Well, he didn't like it that he was being kicked out of his spot. He didn't like it even more when he found out that they've only been working for about three months. So instead of just dealing with it, he said that he wanted to get out. So I said, 'Whatever, but you're never going to come back.' And ever since then he had a grudge against your parents. Then I heard that your parents were found dead."

It was hard for me to take in everything for he was talking so fast, but I think I got the basics. M2 got jealous because my parents knocked him down in command. "So you didn't kill my parents?"

"What?"

"The night that my parents died or never came home, they got a call supposedly from you saying that there was an emergency meeting. Then the next day, you set me half a million doors as well as a note saying that my parents were good partners but they made one big mistake."

Mandel looked at me. "Natalie, I don't have proof that I didn't kill them, but all I can do is give you my word."

I nodded. "Then I will accept it?"

CHAPTER 11

I was glad that I could trust Mandel and know that he didn't have anything to do with my parents' death. However, I still wondered if he knew something he wasn't telling me. However again, I wouldn't be surprised if he would tell me something new. For the past few months have been nothing but surprises.

The next morning came fast. Too fast. I woke up in a bed not my own. At first, I forgot what happened and wondered why I was in one of the guest rooms. Then I remembered what happened.

I also remembered that Mandal said that us three—Carlos, Alistair, and I—were going to go to boot camp. Or in his words, mini-boot camp. I got dressed and headed downstairs for breakfast.

I walked down the stairs slowly to evaluate the house. I didn't know why, but something was wrong. It didn't seem the same. I stopped then thought about it until I realized that I always came down the south wing stairs, and I was coming down the east wing.

I headed into the kitchen to help myself to some grapefruit. Soon I was joined by Alistair who, by the look of it, wasn't really excited for today. He wasn't smiling like usual, his shirt was backward, and he had two different sneakers on.

"Good morning," Carlos said as he entered the room. He went over to Alistair and slapped his back while saying, "Hello, my good, sweet *awake* brother."

Alistair gave him a look to back off, but Carlos didn't even budge or make an attempt to move. However, finally he walked away from him and came over to me. Carlos put his arm around my shoulder. "I can tell we are very happy this morning," he said.

I smiled as I pushed off his arm. "Do you guys want some eggs?" I asked.

They shrugged their shoulders. "Sure," Alistair said.

"Okay, I'll make three," I agreed.

Alistair and Carlos went out of the room to go feed the horses. They had a bet with one of the maids that they could do a better job.

I went over to the fridge when Henrietta, the cook, came in. She had a scared look on her face as if something happened. "Is something wrong?" I asked.

"I hope you don't mind. I thought that I would make Carlos, Alistair, and me some breakfast," I said again.

She smiled then sighed. "Oh, miss, I can do that for you."

"No, no, you go rest. If Master Mandel asks for an explanation, say that Miss Natalie told you to do so. Okay?"

A thankful smile crossed her face. "Yes, thank you, Miss Natalie. I am most grateful."

I watched her leave as I opened the door to the fridge. I took out three eggs and set them on an egg tray as I got out the pan.

I made two eggs already. Two for both Alistair and me. As I was making the last one for Carlos, I looked to my left and saw Hot Sauce #1. I knew I shouldn't have, but I couldn't help myself. I took the cap off and poured some of it in the pan with the rest of the eggs.

I mixed it in really well, and then when they were done, I put them on a plate like I did with the rest. I was really careful to make sure that I didn't mix up any of the plates.

I called them, Carlos and Alistair, to the table to eat. Only when I called them, Mandel showed up with them. He didn't sit down but stayed standing there when the three of us sat down. "Morning, Natalie," Mandel said to me.

"Good, morning," I said back.

"You didn't make me any eggs."

"Well, I didn't know you wanted some," I said to Mandel while smiling.

"Whatever. I'll just have some of Carlos's, seeing that Alistair managed to stuff it all down already."

Alistair smiled.

Mandel took the fork from the table. "Oh, and look, I get the first bite."

"They were good," Alistair said.

Mandel poked the food and made it stay on the fork while he moved it up to his mouth.

"NO!" I yelled.

The three of them froze and stared at me. "What is wrong with you?" Carlos asked.

I looked at Carlos then at Mandel. "Oh . . . nothing."

Mandel smiled and started to put the forkful of food in his mouth. I clenched my fists and closed my eyes, scared of what might happen. I felt like running off.

I watched him with attentive eyes as he put the food in his mouth and chewed. As he swallowed, he looked at me with a face. I was scared. I never saw that face before. "Umm, very spicy, but in any case, good. Good job, Natalie."

I looked at him then at Carlos. He was looking at me with a raised eyebrow. "Um, thanks."

"I guess I won't be eating breakfast," Carlos said as Mandel took his plate and began eating.

I looked my plate. I didn't even start eating. "You could have mine, but I ate it already," Alistair said, smiling.

Carlos gave him a face. "You can have mine," I told him.

At first, he didn't budge but then just got up and went into the kitchen. I didn't know what he was doing until he came out with a plate of eggs. He looked at me, "I didn't trust you. You could have put something in there."

Everyone started laughing. "I'll take your eggs," Alistair said while looking at me.

"No, you don't have time, Carlos, finish it then come up to my study," Mandel said to Alistair, yet at Carlos.

Alistair and I followed Mandel to his study. Now what?" I asked.

"Now, you get your uniforms," Mandel answered me.

"Oh, okay."

Once we got in the room and the three of us sat down, the door opened, and in walked Carlos. "Am I late?" was his first question.

"No, actually you're right on time," Mandel informed him.

He sat down in a chair right across from me. "Now, since we are all here, I will get started. I told you a yesterday that I am putting you three in what I would like to call boot camp. Now these are your uniforms. I know that you, Natalie, wouldn't like the shirts so I have a tank top for you," he said as he turned around and bent down to pick up three sets of outfits.

The shirts were brown, and the pants were camouflage. He gave the boys the ones with the regular T-shirts and handed me the one with the tank.

"You will start tomorrow morning. But in order to do that, you must get there first."

I looked at him with confused eyes. "What do you mean, *we gotta get there first?* I thought this was going to be right here at home."

He shook his head. "No, you will be going to Livani. It is west of Malta. Don't worry, it's only for a week. Now if I were you, I would go to your rooms and get your things together. The plane leaves in three hours."

The three of us, Carlos, Alistair, and I, looked at each other, got up, and headed for the door.

We went to our rooms and got packed as he suggested. I went into my room. It was cleaner than it was the day before, but some things were still out of place. I went and got a duffle bag and put in my socks and personal things. (You don't need to know that stuff.)

I zipped up my belongings and threw it over my shoulder. I walked toward the door. I walked through the halls to the staircase and walked downstairs. Alistair, Carlos, and Mandel were waiting for me. "You take much longer than a boy," Carlos informed me.

"Maybe, but we get the job done right," I said back.

He looked at me with a face to show that he didn't get it but then laughed. "Well then."

Mandel budded in with "All right, you too. Now, time to go." Just as he got done talking, Yassen came into the room. "Yassen will take you to Livani."

Yassen bowed and smiled. "Come on, you three. We better go."

We followed him to the door. I looked back and waved good-bye to Mandel, and he smiled and said, "*Bye,* dear."

I smiled and turned to walk again, but inside, I was shocked that he called me "dear." I was never called that, even when my parents were alive.

We walked out of the house in a single file. We wouldn't have, but Yassen said that we better get used to it for we would do that a lot once in Livani anyway.

We got in the car. And I mean a car, not a limo like I normally would have. At first I was shocked. But then I realized that I was getting way too spoiled. I remember back to when that was the type of car. It was a 2007 Honda. I think, anyway, I was never very good at cars.

Well, we got in the car then headed to the airport. It was a quiet ride. "So what do you wanna talk about?" I said, trying to break the silence.

Carlos looked at me and said, "Let's talk about how bad we are going to be."

I knew he was talking about how good we were going to be once we start our training at boot camp. And I couldn't help but agree with him. The only person who was going to be really good was Alistair.

CHAPTER 12

We reported to the airport prior to the time that we were taking off. Yassen showed us the way. As we were walking through the buildings, people were looking at us left and right; they knew who we were.

"Why are they staring at us?" I asked Alistair.

"The Mafia is really known for doing business in Livani. Don't worry, they're scared of you. Just walk with your head held high," Alistair told me.

I did what he said, my head was held high, and I was walking swiftly next to them.

Once we were in the port that we had to be in to wait for the plane, we sat down. Yassen went over to get us registered for half of the first class to ourselves. While he was doing that, a man came over to us and stood right in front of me. "Well, what do we have here? Now there is a girl in the Mafia. Wow, what do you do? Bring to food to everyone?" the man said loud enough for everyone to hear. Everyone around us looked at us.

"Sir, I would like it if you just walked away right now," I said politely.

When he didn't, Alistair stood up and crisscrossed his arms. "I don't think you heard her. Because if you did, then you would have done what she told you to do. I think she told you to leave. However, she said it politely, if you don't do it this time, I will remind you, but I won't be polite. Make a choice. Either you get out of our faces or you can deal with me."

The man looked at Carlos, Alistair, and me. Then he left. As he walked away, he looked back at me. He pointed at me then at himself and then he took his right hand, put it in a fist, and slammed it on his left palm.

I took in a deep breath. "Thanks," I told Alistair as he sat back down.

"Sure. You get used to that. People always treat us differently."

"I wonder who that guy was," Carlos said, budding in.

"I don't have a clue, but I don't know about you guys, but I don't feel like running after him to ask."

Carlos and Alistair nodded in agreement.

By the time Yassen came back, everything was cool or, in other words, we were calmed down. "So did everything go okay?" Yassen asked as he was walked our way.

When he got to us, the loud speaker stated that our plane was ready for us so we could start boarding. The three of us got up and started to walk out in front of him. "Don't worry about it, *Yassy*, we took care of it," I said as I walked passed him and tapped the back of his left shoulder.

As he started to follow us, he whispered to himself, "Yassy?"

We walked shoulder to shoulder. I was in the middle. Our eyes were forward, not looking left or right. At first I thought that it was a little weird, but Carlos said that people would get out of our way if we did that.

I am not going to say it happened, but out of the corner of my eye, I thought I saw some man raise his arm up and say, "Hail Hitler."

I quickly turned my head to see where Yassen was. He was walking right behind us, looking straight ahead as we were. I could tell that he was proud of us. He had a smile on his face. It was a hard smile. But when did I ever see him give a soft one?

We half-marched all the way to the plane entrance. When we got there, the guards had us show them anything that we had as they did to all the others. Then we waited in line for the metal detector. They had us take off our show and put anything that we were carrying (carry-on, etc) in a small box. That was then taken away through a conveyor belt. After that, we were commanded to walk *slowly* through the metal detector.

The four of us walked through the open doorway (the detector). Once we were ready to grab our bags and leave to the tunnel, a bag detector went off, and everyone was told not to go anywhere. They scanned up and down the rows until they came to us. The security demanded to open up the bags that we were carrying. They opened up all of ours. "Is this all of your luggage that you're taking on the plane?" the security guard asked.

"That case," Yassen said while pointing to a medium-sized brown leather case on the conveyor belt.

Alistair, Carlos, and I looked at each other in confusion. We didn't remember seeing that case.

The guard walked over toward the case while pushing us aside. He opened it up. It was a gun case. I could feel watching eyes on us.

He pulled out four Glock handguns. Everyone who was watching backed off and went once again about their business. "Sir, is this really necessary?" the guard asked Yassen.

"If you don't think so, you are free to call Lar Mandel," Yassen said.

Apparently, the guard knew who Lar Mandel was because he looked at all of us and cleared his throat. "No, as long as you have an adequate reason for carrying it, you may have it."

Yassen shook hands with the man and carried the gun case while starting to walk away.

"Are we going on the plane now?" I asked Carlos.

"Yeah, as soon as we get past all of the people, we are allowed to start boarding," he told me.

"What do you mean we can start boarding as soon as we get past the people?" I asked. I knew that it was a stupid question, but I was in a stupid mood.

"Are you serious? You're asking me why we have to get past the people? I don't think I'm even going to answer that."

He patted my shoulder and walked up to catch up with the others. I gave a silent chuckle and rushed to reach the rest of the gang.

"Natalie, will you please try to keep up with us," Yassen commanded to me as I was trying to catch up.

"What's wrong, Yassen? All of a sudden you're, like, mean," Alistair asked, defending me.

Yassen stopped in his tracks. He looked behind him to face me. "I'm sorry for being so *desolate* and *gloomy*, but from here on out until we are in this very building to head back home, I am to be your commanding officer. You will address me as sir. Then after you are done with your mini-boot camp, then we will become pals again. Okay?"

He then faced the boys to express that he was talking to them to. "Now come, let us hurry before we miss our flight."

His little speech made me feel somewhat degraded. We weren't all one now. It was Alistair, Carlos, and me as one. And Yassen was like the odd ball. If this was what boot camp was all about, I didn't think I was going to like it.

Yassen put his arm around my shoulder as we continued once again to our plane's entrance. "Flight A 96, Livani is now boarding. Repeating Flight A 96, Livani is now boarding. Please make your way to the boarding tunnel," said the loud speaker.

Once again, we made our way down the airport. Once we got to the boarding, tunnel two guards in blue uniforms ordered us to show our passports. When we showed him our identity and our plan tickets, he let us in to go to our seats.

The seat order was Yassen out the outside, Carlos, and then Alistair, who was next to me. Lucky me, I got the window seat.

We waited about fifteen more minutes until the surround system announced, "We will be taking off shortly. Please fasten your seatbelts."

So we all buckled up. I stared out of the window. Soon we started to turn around to face the runway. We started out slow, but then we went faster, faster, and faster. It was loud. When it started to go up, everyone made a *whoa* sound.

When we were just about up or just about done going up, my ear started to pop. It hurt. Since it was my first time flying, I was at first a little freaked out about it. But once I was used to it, I thought it was boring.

For the first hour, I didn't do anything but stare out the window. But then it started to get a little boring. And we still had about three hours to go. Then some stewardess came down our isle. "Would you like a reader?" one lady asked me.

"Oh, thank you," I replied.

She handed me a magazine then handed me a cup of tea. I looked for somewhere to put them on. Then I looked in front of me, and there was a little white pull-out table. I pulled it and put my tea on it.

I opened up my magazine. *Things Today*, the one subject heading read. *Latest news on the Mafia Industry. Sir Lar Mandel, the head of the Mafia, is said to be taking in a late employee's daughter. And is taking his two sons and her to Livani to be sent to boot camp. Some say that the girl, Natalie, and his son Alistair are lovers. Who knows?*

After I read what they said about me and Alistair, I put the magazine away. I then called for a stewardess to come by and give me another magazine. "Yes, miss," said a lady when she came to me.

"May I have another magazine please?" I asked.

She smiled and handed me another one. I thanked her, and she headed off to continue her job. I looked at the front. *What Not to Do.* I looked at the title again. What not to do? This has got to be interesting. I then looked at what it said about it. *Number 1: Never try to jump off a plane while it's in motion. Number 2: If you're hurt, don't panic. You could go into shock. Number 3: If you are reading this, do not think that this is stupid because there are really people who don't know this.*

I took in a deep breath, trying to think about what I just read. Yeah, it was weird but kind of—I don't know—interesting.

I continued to flip through the pages. I was almost at the last page when a text that read "Sir Alistair Mandel" caught my eye. I looked at it. It gave a whole description on him. And then there was a fan club section where girls put in what they thought about him. I know you really don't want to know what they said, but I'll tell you anyway:

Alistair:
Hair: Brown   Eyes: Brown

Then a girl named Stacy said, "*I think Alistair is, like, the hottest guy that I ever saw. I wish I could be his girlfriend. But then again with his standards, I don't think that anyone could be good enough for him.*"

I rolled my eyes. I wondered if I was good enough for him. I didn't know. But honestly, I didn't know if I wanted to know. I was scared of his answer. He would probably see that I was.

There was more, but I didn't want to know what other girls thought about him. "Hey, what's up?" I heard Carlos ask me.

I almost jumped. Well, I didn't jump, but you could tell that I was startled. I didn't even notice, but Alistair wasn't sitting next to me anymore. He was talking to some chick. And as for Yassen, he went to the lavatory to get something out of his teeth.

"Who is Alistair talking to?" I asked Carlos with a curious face.

Carlos smiled, almost happy that I asked. He quickly sat down on the seat next to me. "Well, it just so happens that they know each other. And she is going to come to boot camp with us."

My shoulders dropped, and my mouth went open a little. "Excuse me. No, she is not. What's her name anyway?

"I'm not going to say, but I think it's Rachel."

At first, I just looked at him because what he just said didn't make any sense, but then I just shrugged. "Hum, well, I think I just might go say hi to *my boyfriend,* if you would excuse me."

I got up and dropped the magazine on Carlos's lap. Unfortunately, the page that I was reading about was on the front page.

I walked over nicely and calmly, trying to think about what I was going to say. When I finally got a good look at her, I couldn't believe it. Perfect blond hair. Perfect body. And her teeth were as white as anything I had ever seen.

I knew I could go up there looking like this. I looked over at Alistair, he had that smile on his face. A girl has to do what a girl has to do. I think anyway. I marched up and said, "Hello, Alistair, I was wondering where you were." Didn't know what I was thinking when I said that, but that Rachel girl was just staring at me.

"And who might this be?" Rachel asked Alistair while looking at me.

Alistair looked at me, "This is . . ."

"I am Natalie, I'm his girlfriend, also part of the Mafia," I said before he could say anything.

Rachel looked at Alistair then at me. "Oh, well, I'm Rachel."

I looked at her. She looked back at me. "I already know that. So I hear that you will be coming to boot camp with us, eh?"

She smiled, "Yes. Alistair invited me, and it just so happened for me to be open."

I returned her smiled. "Oh, isn't that just perfect."

Alistair looked back to where Carlos was sitting. "Carlos, can I talk to you in private."

Carlos nodded, and Alistair and he walked to another seat. "If this is about Rachel and Natalie, let me tell it to you plain and simple. They both like you," Carlos informed his confused brother.

Alistair looked at Carlos then at Rachel. "He's not yours," she told me in a very disturbing manner.

"Well, I had him before you did so deal with it," I told her right back. "Why are you going along to boot camp with us. You're not part of the Mafia."

She smirked as if she were special. "Oh, I don't need to be in the Mafia to go with you. Alistair asked me to. So there. If he didn't like me, then why would he ask me to go along?" she asked in a very convincing tone.

Then back to Carlos and Alistair's little chat. "See? Look at them. They're like yelling," Carlos said while using hand motions. "Dude, she's your sister, don't worry. As soon as Natalie finds out, she'll be totally cool."

Alistair sighed. "I guess I shouldn't have invited Rachel to join us at boot camp, huh?"

Carlos sighed too. He smiled and put his hand on his brother's shoulder as a sign of encouragement. "I don't think it was a good idea."

Alistair made a geeky smile and looked over at us girls. "Well, do you think I should go over to them?"

Carlos looked over at the girls to make up his mind to Alistair's question. "Um, well, you can."

Alistair at first struggled to get up. (I don't mean that he was physically unable. I mean he was scared.)

Me and *Rachel* were just glaring at each other. "Well, I'm glad that you two got a chance to get to know each other," Alistair said while making a fake smile.

I looked at him. "Very funny," I glared at him then walked back to my seat. Soon, Yassen came back from the lavatory.

He sat down and looked at me. "So what did I miss?"

I looked back at him with a serious face. "Yassen, I have only one thing to say."

He nodded for me to go on. "If that girl so much as bothers me, I will dispose of her."

Yassen gave me a puzzled look. "Whoever do you mean by *that girl*? What girl?"

I looked over in the direction of Rachel and spat, "That girl."

Rachel was chatting with Alistair. This time, he was a little bit more hesitant when he smiled. "You mean Rachel?" Yassen questioned.

"Yes."

"Why? What did she do to you?"

"She took my boyfriend. *And* she thinks she can run me over in a sense of saying that she thinks she can tell me what to do."

Yassen nodded his head as if he were taking this all in. "Well, did you tell Alistair about this?"

I shook my head. "Well, I would say you better. If not, you will be dealing with Rachel for about three weeks."

With that, he got up and went to another seat for the rest of the trip. I looked out the window and thought about what he said.

I smiled jealously and whispered, "Alistair, do you think I could talk to you elsewhere?"

I could see his apprehension or his fear of talking to me. "Certainly. Excuse us, please." He told Rachel in a dreamy, pleasant tone of voice.

I walked in the direction that I wanted to talk to him it. "Okay, now what's this all about?" he asked.

I decided to go straight to the point. "I don't want her along."

He smirked before he spoke. I could tell that he wasn't very . . . how should you say . . . *thrilled.* "And what is it that you want exactly?"

I sighed. I stood up straight and tall, hoping that it would help. "I told you, I don't want her along."

"Well, I do so deal with it."

He started to walk away when I yelled. "Fine, then we're over. You can have her as you girlfriend!"

Everyone suddenly became quiet and looked at me. Alistair stopped in his tracks. Then he turned in the opposite direction and walked back to me. "What did you say?"

He grabbed my arm in a sense of defense. I struggled to get loose, but it was useless. He was clearly stronger than me. I was a little bit hesitant before I spoke. "I . . . I . . . I said it was over. If you want to be like that and not care at all about me, then you can treat Rachel like that, but leave me out of it."

I felt quite proud of myself talking to him like that. He gradually relived pressure in my arm. I swear I could see that blood flow again as if it were trapped by the great deal of pressure Alistair betrayed on me.

"We will talk about this later, and until then, we are still going out." While he was saying that, he had his hand on my waist.

He then walked away and continued to talk to Rachel. I conclusion, I just went back to doing what I was, looking out the window from my seat.

To think I thought that I would get married to this guys sometime. Hum, I don't think that's going to happen.

Chapter 13

Indeed he did talk to me about it later, but that was when we landed and we were on our way to the camp. We were in the limo. Alistair and I had one to ourselves and Carlos, Rachel, and Yassen got one for the three of them. To tell you the truth, I didn't really get the concept of having limos to go to boot camp when you were trying to learn how to defend yourself and get tough. But I guess there's a reason for everything.

Inside the limo it was quiet. "So why did you have us get one to ourselves?" I asked quietly.

He looked at me with his soft eyes, which somehow comforted my feelings on the matter. "We need to talk, Natalie," he said at last.

"Well, I agree. Only I considered that method a long time ago. Unfortunately, you didn't."

He sighed and slid over to sit next to me. "Yes, well, now about Rachel. She's my sister."

I couldn't help it. I cracked up laughing. "You have got to be kidding me. What were you two planning? Incest?"

Apparently, he didn't find it as funny as I did. "I'm not laughing," he said in a tone that clearly stated that he really didn't think that it was funny.

"Are you serious? She's really your sister?"

He nodded. "I didn't see her for the last couple of years. Last I heard, she was working with M2. She said that she was done with that and moving on in her life."

I looked down, embarrassed. "So you don't like her?"

He looked at me funny. "Where did you get an idea like that?"

"Naturally, I'm a girl, which makes me naturally curious. And seeing the way you were looking at her . . ."

He shook his head in a way that made me think I was wrong. "You thought that about me? I thought you trusted me."

I felt bad. You know. Didn't you ever accuse someone for something, but then you found out that they were actually innocent? Well, if you did, that's how I felt.

There was an odd silence in the car then. Neither one of us spoke until we got to the camp. The driver opened the door for us, and we got out.

Yassen showed our huts, or cabins, that we were going to be staying in. It just so happened that we were doing a boys' cabin and girls' cabin so I was stuck bunking or hanging out with Rachel. Not that I didn't mind exactly. Not that I understood what was going on, but I felt kind of awkward.

"So you're Natalie," a voice came from behind me.

Without turning, I knew it was Rachel for two reasons. Number 1: she's the only other girl around; and number 2: I knew the guys were over in their cabins.

"Yeah," I said, without looking at her.

She sighed. "I'm Alistair's sister. I think you misjudged me to be someone else."

This time, I did turn a little to look at her. I put on a soft smile. "Yeah, I did. I'm sorry, I didn't mean to be nasty or spiteful. It's just... I'm his girlfriend, and I got jealous. But now I understand."

She smiled, and I turned back around to get the uniform. "I'm going to go change."

I went into the bathroom change into my uniform, which was camouflage khaki pants and a dark green or brown tank top.

I came out of the bathroom, and Rachel was gone. I went out of the small building to see her and Yassen talking. They seemed very comfortable talking to each other as if they've known each other for years. (But how was that? Yassen only came to work with Mandel for two years that Rachel went to work with M2. They didn't see each other no more that once or twice in the last five years.)

I stood there watching them talk until I saw Yassen look over at me. Then I just returned back to the cabin.

We had about two hours to relax and take it easy before we started our training. I was on my bed reading a book on self-defense when Rachel walked in. "Man, it's getting hot out there." I saw her rummage through her duffle bag and get out her uniform, which she still needed to put on.

"You have half an hour before we need to report to start training," I informed her.

"Thanks" was all she said before she entered the bathroom.

I don't know why, but for some reason, I waited for her before I went out to get information. We walked out and over to the big old tree stump, which was where everyone else was.

We stood in a straight line. Yassen had the uniform on as well. "I know that this is a small group, and that it's only us for three weeks," he started. "But I think we will all learn a lot in these three weeks. I will try not to be too *rough*, but I need to be firm so if you notice a change, please understand that this in only temporary, and then I will go back to being my normal self."

We all knew not to say anything, but we did nod.

(In my personal opinion, this was stupid. I mean, the way Yassen was acting. *"I'll try not to be too rough?"* That is so lame. But I need to do this.)

"Now let's all warm up with a five-mile hike."

I never really was good at running, but I had a feeling that by the time this thing was over, running a mile would be a snap.

We all picked up the packs that were assigned to us. Then one by one, we started to jog.

We ran a little trail in the woods. It was pretty. I think I even saw a deer or two. Fifteen minutes into the hike, Rachel jogged up to me. "You wanna talk?" she asked me with a smile.

I didn't want to because it would only make it harder to run, but hesitantly, I said, "Yeah, sure. But what's there to talk about?"

"A lot of things. Um, what do you like to do on your spare times?"

I had to think about that one. I never really did anything. "Well, I like to read if it's an interesting book, um . . ." I had to stop talking for a minutes to catch my breath, "And talk to friends if there are any around."

I could tell she was a little excited. "Really, wow that's so cool. I'm like that too. If the book's not interesting, forget having me read it. And other than that, I'm quiet unless my friends are around. And frankly, I don't have many."

I didn't know why she was so excited just because we had something in common. "Yeah, ain't that something?" I said, trying to sound enthused.

We didn't talk for a while but concentrated on where we were going. I didn't know what to make of Rachel. At first, I was mad at her because I thought she was cheating with my boyfriend. But then I found out that she was *only* Alistair's sister. I mean, I think she is nice now. But in the end, I found that all I think about her is that she is annoying. She started talking to me again, but I didn't pay any attention.

"You listening to me?" she said once she realized that I wasn't.

"Oh, yeah, yeah. Of course."

She shook her head as she ran. "Then what did I say?"

I looked around with my eyes. "Um, I forget."

"That's what I thought. I asked if you like my brother."

Asking if I like her brother (meaning Alistair) was the question that all siblings ask to make sure their brother or sister wasn't being cheated on. "Yeah, of course, I like him. Why do you ask?"

Before Rachel was able to answer, Yassen stopped and we did the same. "Okay, let's take a one-hour brake," he said. I could see him trying to catch his breath.

"Oh, just asking," Rachel then said.

I looked over at Alistair and Carlos. Alistair saw me and motioned for me to go over to him. I walked over, and Rachel openly followed me. "You tired yet?" he asked me.

"Nah."

Alistair looked over at Rachel. "So you two getting along okay?"

Rachel looked over at me before she responded. "Well, your girlfriend has a confessing problem. But other than that, yeah, we're great."

My mouth dropped open. I turned to look at her. Her eyes were full of innocence, but inside, I knew that she was nothing but a little beast. "You little wretch!"

She looked at me. "Excuse me, what did you call me?"

I smiled then turned to Alistair. "I might have a confessing problem, but at least I can hear, unlike you sister *Rachel*. Who in fact appears to be deaf."

I started to walk away. But sure enough, I felt a small yet boney hand grab my shoulder. The hand spun me around. By now the guys were backing away. They didn't want at all to get involved in a chick fight.

"You shouldn't have said that," Rachel said with her hand on my shoulder.

"Oh, and what are you going to do?"

She made a smile that I never saw before. She didn't know what she was going to do. "I will punch you."

I made a little chuckle. "Okay, then do it."

I pointed with my finger right on my lip. Then waited for her to hit me. I closed my eyes. I really didn't think that she was going to do it, but she did. After a couple of seconds, I felt a hard, boney fist pound into my lower lip.

I opened my eyes to see Rachel looking at me. As soon as she saw blood drain from my lip, she smiled. "See, I said that I was going to hit you, and I did."

Even though it didn't hurt, I gave her the benefit of a doubt and just nodded. "But I still say that you're deaf."

I slapped her across the face and walked away a little faster than the first time. I didn't slap her hard enough to make her cry, but instead it was a warning that if she does it again, I will take action.

CHAPTER 14

I walked all the way back to camp and into the little mess hall (eating room) to get a towel with ice. Even though getting hit in the face by Rachel didn't hurt, I knew that I would definitely feel it the next day.

I was dabbing my bruised face when Yassen came in. They all came back. I gave him a mellow smile.

He walked toward me with a lenient smile in return. "That was some conversation out there. You all right?" he asked me.

I shrugged. "Yeah, no sweat."

I looked out of the window. "I want to warn you. Rachel used to work with Mandel #2 that's why we didn't see her for, like, years."

I turned to give him my full attention. "And?"

"And just be careful. She still might be with him."

I nodded to say thank you. Then in a blink of an eye, he was gone. I smiled to myself and continued to dab my face.

Once I was done, I went back outside. The guys were helping Yassen with some things, but when I looked for Rachel, she was nowhere to be seen. "Hey guys, have you seen Rachel?" I asked.

They stopped to look at me. "No, she said that she was going to go and get some wood," Carlos said.

I took in a deep breath. "When did she leave?"

Alistair looked at his watch. "Um, about an hour ago," he answered.

"Isn't that a little long to be out looking for firewood. I mean, there's a ton right around here. And why did she need some anyway? It's not like we need a fire for another couple of hours. And we have light in the cabins."

Yassen had a look of worry on his face. "I think we should go find her."

I nodded. "Let's split up. Carlos and I will go this way," I said, pointing in the direction that I was referring to. "And you and Alistair can go that way."

We split up to look for who was and who might still be a traitor. "Rachel," we yelled for hours.

Finally, we heard a gunshot, we all ducked down. We didn't know who was shooting. We didn't know a lot of things. However, we did know that Rachel has not been around for about five years because she was working with Mandel #2 (the enemy), and now she shows up for boot camp but then disappears and we hear gunshots. I don't know what that means. Maybe you can understand it.

When we didn't hear anything for about five minutes, we stood up and started looking once again.

Soon we heard a rustling in the bushes. We stopped and became silent. We looked around. Carlos tapped my shoulder and pointed at the direction that the noise came from. There got up Rachel. She was covering her left arm with her right hand. Blood was running down her arm.

I looked at her; she made a soft smile. I smiled too then started to step toward her. I had my hand stretched out like you would to a wild animal. I stepped closer when Carlos moved.

Rachel's attention then moved to Carlos. She had fear in eyes, for sure afraid of us. (I don't know why, she had the courage to hit me.)

Surely she knew that we wouldn't hurt her. The only person that she was around in the last couple of years was M2.

Rachel kept looking back at us. Then in came from behind us Alistair and Yassen. "Oh, you found her," Yassen said to us.

I nodded but kept my eye on her. "Rachel, who shot you?" I asked her.

"Was it . . . ."

I didn't need to finish, she nodded. We both knew that it was Mandel #2.

"Rachel, where is he?"

It took her a while before she answered. Apparently, the three guys didn't know who we were talking about because they were whispering.

"Where is he, Rachel? I'm not playing games."

She gulped. I could see that she was in pain. Tears started to roll down her face. She went down on her knees.

She looked up at me. Everything was silent. She sniffled. "Rachel, I'm only going to ask you once more. Where is he?"

She looked down on the dirt that she was sitting on. Then met my eyes. She opened her mouth when a noise swept the camp.

We looked around when out from behind the trees came a chopper. And in that chopper was *him*. "Everyone, down," Alistair yelled.

We dived to the earth's floor. I covered Rachel. At first, it was silent except for the noise of the flying metal bird. But then all of a sudden, we heard nothing but guns being shot from the air in our direction. We ducked down harder.

This went on for five more minutes then it went silent and the metal bird left. We got up off the ground and brushed ourselves off.

Then Carlos and I turned back over to Rachel to help her up. Her eyes were closed, and her hand was away from her bruised arm. Yassen made his way to her. He looked at her. Her body just laid there. He picked her up.

"Let's take her back to camp and get that arm fixed up," he said.

We followed him back to camp. Which was quite a long way. Since we were looking for her for about an hour. We kind of wandered off into the woods quite aways.

Finally, when we got back to the camp, we went into one of the cabins and laid her on one of the cots.

"Go and get my bag. You know, the one with all the knives. Don't forget the first aid," Yassen told Carlos.

Carlos nodded and went to do what he was told. While he was gone doing that, Yassen went to wash his hands. Then he asked me to rip her shirt up to her left shoulder.

Soon, he came back, and Carlos was right behind him. It was only a flesh wound. You know, when there's a scrape on the skin. Well it's more than just a scrape, it's deeper.

First, Yassen cleaned the wound then took one of his sharpest knives to get the cloth out of her arm. (To explain this to you, when the bullet hit Rachel's arm, it went past her left shoulder, grazing it while making some of her shirt got, embedding in her arm) Then he sterilized it again. As soon as he was done with all that, he put a bandage around it.

"Now, let us go and have her rest."

We left then. Once we were back outside, Carlos said, "Now what are we going to do?"

Alistair looked at him. "About what?"

"Now that we know that M2 is here, we don't know when he's going to pay us a little visit."

Yassen sighed. "We can't do anything. We can only do what we are here for. We will continue to train, and when *he* comes, we can only hope that we are ready. But if we just wait, he'll never come because he'll *know* that we're ready."

We all nodded in agreement. For the rest of the day, Yassen got us doing pushups and what-nots.

We were jogging around the camp when Yassen came over to get Alistair. "Sir, it's for you," he said while handing over a phone.

Alistair stopped went into a little hut to talk. "Yes, I'm listening," he echoed.

There was a long silence before the other line started to talk. "I will get you. How much do you like your girlfriend? Would you risk your life for her?" the mysterious voice said.

Alistair looked straight ahead and leaded on a beam that was up against the wall. "If you ever go as much as thirty feet from Natalie, I will get you, which won't be too hard since you keep contacting us," he answered back.

What he said didn't really make any sense, but when you're mad and all you wanna do is beat the crap out of someone, not everything that you say will make sense.

Alistair came out of the hut then and gave the phone back to Yassen.

He joined us once again to our thirty-minute workout. This workout included kicks, punches, and, well, that's pretty much it. But I wasn't doing it. I was taking a break.

"Who was that?" Carlos asked.

Alistair didn't answer him at first but started on his workout again.

"Well, who was it?" I asked to see if he would answer me.

He didn't stop what he was doing but just said, "Someone."

I threw my hands up. The thing with Alistair that I observed was that if he didn't want to tell you something, it didn't matter what you did, he wouldn't talk. I got up from the log that I was sitting on. "Okay, I'm done," I said to Yassen.

"What do you mean?" Yassen asked me back.

"I mean that I'm done exercising. I'm going to go back into my little hut and read."

I walked away then. I could hear them talking about me, but I didn't bother to turn around and harass them so I just let it go.

CHAPTER 15

I basically stayed in that hut for the next couple of days. I didn't feel like talking to no one (or training, for that matter). I remember yesterday, Carlos came in and asked if I would like to do something. My answer was no. Then this morning, Alistair asked the same thing. I looked at him and shook my head.

It was around lunchtime when Yassen came in. "Natalie, Rachel's up," he said.

He walked over from the door to the side of my bed. He sat down and looked at me. "Don't you wanna talk to her?"

I looked down then to the side. I did but didn't feel like it. I shrugged then moved my feet onto the floor. Yassen smiled and showed me to her. She was in one of the empty huts (so she has it peaceful and quiet. What's not peaceful about me?).

I first knocked on the door then made my way in. "Rachel," I said.

At first, I couldn't see her, but then she put her head up. "Hey," she said. I could tell she wasn't exactly happy to see me, but I didn't care.

I walked over to her bed. "May I?"

She nodded and I sat down. "So how's it going?"

She shrugged. "It's going."

I looked around. What was I supposed to talk to her about?

"Your arm okay?"

"Sure."

I sighed. "Okay, Rachel, you're going to tell me about it." She looked at me, puzzled. "I know you know what I'm talking about."

She looked away at first then spoke, "You're talking about in the woods, a couple of days ago, aren't you?"

"Well, if you're talking of the incident a couple of days ago when M2 tried to kill you, yes, I am talking about that. So you wanna tell me about that?"

Rachel looked down at her hands, clutching the cloth of her blanket. "He wasn't trying to kill me. He was telling me something. If he wanted to kill me, it would have been a head shot. And he wouldn't have missed."

I looked at her. "What do you think he wants? What was he telling you?" She looked at me. "You can trust me," I assured her.

She nodded. "I know, even though we don't like each other that much. He had left him. He knew that you were going to boot camp. He wanted me to go with you. He said that he'll let me know when he wanted me back."

I shook my head. "Why did he want you to go to boot camp with us. Don't you already know self-defense?"

"If I knew self-defense then, you wouldn't have slapped me. And he wants me back. And back I must go before he does make a head shot. He wanted me to go to boot camp to see . . ."

She stopped and told me no more. "I need to go" was all she said.

I got up and left. I looked back at her before I closed the door. She knew something.

I walked out into the brisk air. I looked up at the blue sky. The clouds moved slowly to the left. I watched the carefully. I remembered when I was young I would sit on a big hill and watch them. I would pretend that they were animals of some sort.

I remained standing there, watching. I smiled, thinking about how the one looked like the head of Carlos.

Just in the nick of time, Carlos came walking my way. He came over next to me and looked in the direction I was smiling at. "Um, what are you doing?" he asked me.

I just smiled a replied. "I'm looking at you."

I knew he didn't understand but that was the funny part of it. "You're what?"

I pointed up at the clouds. "Remember how we would sit on a hill and watch the clouds for hours?"

He looked at me and smiled. "Yeah."

"It seems that those days just disappeared."

Carlos smiled at me. He took my arm and pulled me away. I didn't know where we were going.

We walked past Yassen, and all Carlos said was, "Just us a few hours."

Yassen just shrugged. "Let me tell you one thing. This was supposed to be a tough couple of weeks. Well, this is the easiest boot camp I ever went to."

"Where are we going?" I asked him a multiple of times.

When he never answered me those times I asked, I merely thought that it was a surprise.

And a surprise it was. He brought me out to the open. The grass was green, and the trees swayed in the wind. Up ahead was a big hill. I covered my face with my hand to keep me from smiling. Not that I didn't want to smile. I was just shocked. Well, you know how people get when they're surprised.

He took me up to the top of the hill. We laid down and started up at the sky. Even though I wasn't dating him, this was the sweetest thing that a guy did. Carlos tapped me on the shoulder and pointed up at the sky. "You see it?" he asked.

I nodded and laughed. "Yeah. Do you know who it reminds me of?"

He shook his head. "It reminds me of the girl who used to go to our school. You remember the snobby one, Cassandra?"

Carlos laughed too. "You know, it does. That is so funny. You never did get along, did you? She would always make fun of you because she thought that you were in the Mafia."

We looked at each other. It was quiet. To break the silence, I said, "Yeah, the funny thing is that I'm really part of it now."

He nodded. The we just laid back down and analyzed the clouds for the next hour. Occasionally, we would laugh or make fun of a cloud that looked like someone we knew.

Instead of one, many hours passed. I even think we fell asleep. The only reason I think I got up was because I heard Alistair's voice. I opened my eyes and saw Alistair staring down at me. "Oh, hi. Um, we're looking at clouds," I said.

He smiled. "Yep, come on," he said.

He pulled me up to my feet. I looked over, and Carlos was asleep. How ironic.

"Yassen wants you," he informed me.

I blinked my eyes a little to get awake. "Why does he want me?" I asked while half-yawning.

"Rachel wants to leave, and Yassen thinks that you can talk her out of it."

I shook my head in disagreement. "No, I can't. I talked to her earlier, and she said that it was something that she had to do. And if she doesn't, maybe M2 will make a head shot."

He looked at me with a confused expression when I mentioned the head shot but did ask. "Okay well, I still think you should come back with me, or us, if Carlos decided to get up."

He took my hand and started to walk down the hill. "Shouldn't we tell Carlos that we're going back to the camp?"

Alistair picked up a small rock. He threw it up in the air a couple of times then caught it. He stopped turned around and threw it at Carlos. The rock flew into the air and landed on top of Carlos's stomach. "Hey, what was that for?" Carlos asked while waking up.

"We're heading back the camp, are you coming or staying?" Alistair asked his brother.

Carlos quickly got up off the soft grass floor and ran to catch up with us. "So Carlos, what were you doing out here, alone with my girlfriend?" Alistair asked him, smiling.

"We were remembering how fun it was to be young and watch the clouds go by" was Carlos's answer.

Alistair looked at his brother. "Were you trying to be romantic or something? Because you failed, badly."

I started to walk a little faster. "I don't know. If I was dating him I would have given him a ten," I reminded them.

Carlos gave a chuckle and put his hand on Alistair's shoulder. "Looks like I beat you on this one."

Carlos gave another laugh and ran up to walk next to me. Alistair gave a look of annoyance. Then he walked up and went in the middle of me and Carlos. "Maybe, but I'm still her boyfriend; and you're not."

We all laughed and headed back to Yassen.

We came to about a third of a mile away from the camp. Smoke was everywhere. And by everywhere, I mean, as in, in the air. Resulting to a fire. We ran to see what was going on.

Alistair and Carlos went in the opposite direction than I did to see where everyone was. Normally, there were security guards or something.

I slowed to a slow walk, examining everything. It was a mess. I started to hear a moaning coming from behind one of the huts. I followed it when I found Yassen laying there on the ground. I ran over to his side. He was breathing heavily. I noticed that he was holding his right arm. I pulled his left hand away so I could see what happened. He was grazed with a bullet. It didn't go in him, but it brushed past him and took some of the skin along with it.

Since I didn't have a medical degree, I had no clue on what to do. I put his hand back on his right arm. I got up and went to look for Carlos or Alistair. Or maybe both.

I ran all around until I finally found both of the pouring water over a small patch of fire. "I need your help," I said.

They stopped what they were doing and looked at me. "I found Yassen."

They looked at me. Carlos wiped his face with the back of his dirty hand. "Okay, where is he?" Alistair asked.

Carlos and Alistair followed me to where I found Yassen. With the two of them, they carefully carried Yassen to one of the bed in the huts.

Carlos told me to go and get a bowl of warm water. I didn't know what it was for, but I gave him no trouble. I went and did as he asked.

I brought back what Carlos had asked for. He tried to clean the wound, but it wouldn't stop bleeding. "We need help," Alistair said. "Carlos, go call for help. Natalie and I will help Yassen as much as we can."

Carlos nodded at his brother and left to call someone.

That left us two alone. "Where are all of the guard people?" I asked.

"Well, there were only three guards, but even if they were hurt, they should still be here. I still wonder what happened."

I sighed. "My guess is that Mandel #2 came back for Rachel, and Yassen tried to stop him. Mandel #2 shot Yassen, burned the place, and took the guards."

Alistair nodded. "I like your story. I guess we'll find out as soon as Yassen can talk."

"Yep."

CHAPTER 16

We took a jet home. Once we got Yassen home and in his room, we called for Dr. Hampton. "We don't really know what happened," Carlos and I told the doctor as we walked up to Yassen's room.

"Hum, isn't he talking about it?" the doc asked.

"Well, he is. But doesn't say much. He says that he can't remember what happened," I said.

Dr. Hampton scratched his head. "Oh. Well at least we'll take care of his arm."

Carlos and I nodded in agreement.

We came to Yassen's room when we knocked. "Do you really think I'm going to come and open it for you," a voice said from inside the room, clearly stating it was Yassen.

"Sorry, Yassen thinks he fine so he was getting these moods," Carlos said as he opened the door.

"Hiya, Yassen. So I heard you got into a little accident," the doctor greeted.

"Oh, stop treating me like I'm some kid. Just do what you doctors normally do so I can get back to work. Okay? *Comprendo?*"

Dr. Hampton looked at him then at us. "Yeah, whatever you say. Do you mind telling me what happened?"

The doctor walked over to the sofa and put down his bag. The he took out some bandages and went over to the bed to look at Yassen's arm.

"I forget. All I know is that M2 came, took Rachel, and that's all I remember. So can you just hurry up?"

Dr. Hampton looked at us. "Thanks, guys, I can take it from here."

We both nodded and started to head for the door. "Hey, Carlos, can you tell your father that I'll be fine and ready to get back to work in no time?" Yassen asked him.

Carlos gave him a thumbs-up, and we left the room. "What did he mean by getting back to work? All they do is talk. And to me, that's not exactly what I call work. What do you think?" I asked Carlos.

He shrugged his shoulders. "Beats me. All I wanna know is where Alistair is," he answered back.

We walked down the steps to the study to see Mandel. "Hey, guys," he said as he greeted. "So how was boot camp. Was it as bad as you thought?"

I had to admit. It wasn't as bad as I thought. But it was kind of boring. "I met your daughter. Would you like to tell me about that?" I asked him.

I could tell that Mandel didn't plan on having Rachel join us. "What? When?" His focus turned over to Carlos.

"On the plane. She didn't tell us why she was there though. She and Natalie were having it out. Rachel told her that Alistair asked her to come so Natalie would get mad. However, when we were at the boot camp, she ran away. Then Mandel #2 tried to kill her or was shooting at her for some odd reason," Carlos explained to his father.

"Then I talked to her, and she said that M2 had her come and that he was shooting at her to say that it was time for her to come back," I finished.

Mandel was nodding to everything that we said. "Okay, well, do you two know where Alistair might be?"

We shook our heads. "No, we were going to ask you the same question," I said.

"Well, you two go and look for him. Tell me when you find him. Okay?"

Again, Carlos and I nodded as we headed for the door. "Oh, and father, Yassen wanted me to tell you that he'll be ready for duty soon," Carlos said with half a grin on his face.

"Oh, good," Mandel said, smiling.

"Okay, now where would Alistair be? He's not in his room nor the kitchen or the study," Carlos analyzed.

"Hum, I don't know, maybe he's outside. Yeah, Carlos, I think he might be outside," I said sarcastically.

Carlos rolled his eyes. "Fine, we go outside."

So we went outside. It was warm but getting late. Soon we heard pounding. We followed the noise until we came to the basketball court. Alistair shooting hoops. "We were looking for you," I informed him.

He nodded but continued to shoot hoops. "Okay, what's wrong," Carlos asked his brother.

Alistair gave us the back-off expression. Carlos sighed and started to go back inside. "Aren't you coming?" Carlos asked me.

"Nope, I wanna know what his problem is."

Carlos shrugged his shoulders and continued to head inside. I waited until Carlos was out of sight. Then I made myself over to the bench. "What are you thinking," I asked Alistair as he jogged up and down the court.

"I think that Yassen should go on a vacation," he answered.

My eyes widened. I didn't expect that coming. "Really?"

"Yep."

"And where do you think he should go?"

"Well, not really a vacation but like a mission. But by himself. You know, so he can think and yet work."

I nodded. "Well, that sounds like a good idea."

Hum, I came outside hoping to talk about us, and somehow the conversation turned to having Yassen go on a vacation.

Alistair bounced the ball once again then caught it and held it. "Now why did you really come out here? Surely you didn't really care about where I was."

I got up and walked toward him. "Alistair, I'm your girlfriend. I'm naturally supposed to wonder where you are. If you don't wanna accept that, then that's your choice."

I took the ball from him and started to walk away. Then I stopped and turned around. I quickly aimed and made a three-point shot. I smiled and continued to walk into the house.

When I got inside, I saw Carlos and his father talking. I walked up to Mandel and said, "Alistair and I think that Yassen should go on a mission or vacation."

Mandel stopped talking and looked at me. "Really?"

"Yeah. I mean it would be a good opportunity."

He looked at me. "What opportunity?"

"I don't have a clue. But it would be cool."

"Um, well, does Yassen know about this?"

I raised an eyebrow at him. "If he did, I wouldn't be telling you this now, would I?"

He looked at me, like, "stop it." "Okay, well, I guess we can have him go in a couple of days to a week."

I gave a little shriek of excitement. "Yes!"

Mandel looked at me with curiosity. "Well, it looked like you really want him to go."

"Well, Alistair really wants him to go too so of course I want him to go."

I turned to go tell Yassen the good news. I walked up the stairs and to his room. I knocked on the door before I went in. Then like before, I heard his voice. "Well, come in already."

I smiled to myself and walked in. "Oh, Natalie, it's you," Yassen said, softening his voice.

I smiled and saw Dr. Hampton standing there, taking his pulse. "Yassen, settle down," the doctor kept telling him.

I walk closer to the bed. "Yassen, I have a surprise."

He smiled and looked at me. "What is it?"

I closed my eyes for a moment and breathed in. "If you want to, you may go on a vacation or mission for a week."

I stood there, quietly waiting for him to answer me. He looked at me, studying my eyes. "Hum, well, okay. That sounds good."

I nodded. "Okay, I will go tell Mandel that you agreed."

I nodded again then smiled at the doctor. "Bye," I said.

They both said bye, and I left the room. I walked down the stairs.

Alistair met me halfway down. "So what did he say?" he said as he turned around and headed down with me.

"He said that he would like to," I told him. We came to the bottom of the stairs when we came across Mandel. "Hey," I yelled after him.

I hurried up to him as I saw him stop. Only he stopped before I could, and I sort of bumped into him. He held out his hands to steady me. I felt stupid but it was okay. We were all laughing. "What is it?" he asked me.

I took in a deep breath and let it out. "Yassen says that he'll go."

"Okay, good. Then as soon as he is up to it, he will be going to the Netherlands."

I smiled. "Good."

As you could imagine, Yassen said that he was well enough to go the next day. So as Mandel said, he could go. Personally, I didn't think he was ready. How could you be ready if you still ran into walls?

He gave us all a hug then ran out of the house. "See you back in the next two months or sooner," he yelled as he got into the limo.

Unfortunately, that was going to it of Yassen for the next few days, weeks, maybe months.

Chapter 17

Mandel walked down the halls to my room. He knocked and I answer with a "Yes?" He came in with a smile on his face. "What's going on," I asked curiously.

"Oh, nothing. I was just seeing what you were doing," he said as he put his arms behind his back.

I came off of the bed because I knew something was wrong and I wanted to know what it was.

"Did you need something?"

He shook his head. "I don't need anything. I just wanted to remind you of the meeting that I have, like, in a couple of minutes in town. I won't be home until dark. I would have told one of the boys, but they seem to be in the middle of a video game contest. And as you know, if you tell them anything then, they will surely forget it. So I am telling you so you can tell them. Okay?"

"Um, yeah. Sure thing." I stared at him, puzzled.

He looked at me and through his hand up as if he was a mad scientist and one of his invention didn't work. "No one in this family came from my side of the family. I can tell you that much; no one is smart." He was laughing as he went out the door.

I laughed as well, but then it ended right after he closed the door. I went back over to the bed and continued to read my book. The boys were in a video contest? They never played against each other.

I put my book down and got off my bed once again soon after Mandel left. I walked over to the door and walked out into the hallway. I went downstairs and headed for the back of the house. I looked out of one of the window and saw that Mandel had already gone.

I entered the game room, and Mandel was right. There sat two teenage boys. If you didn't know how old they really were, you would have thought that they were really six-years-olds. Only in big kids' bodies.

"Ha-ha, I got you now," Carlos yelled in a weird defeating voice.

"On the contrary, my dear fellow, you only have one life. And . . . I . . . have . . . killed . . . you," Alistair said.

Alistair threw the controller onto the floor to as a motion to show that he had no intention of doing a redo.

Carlos started murmuring to himself when they both got up. When they turned, they gave an expression that showed they were shocked to see me.

"How long were you standing there?" Carlos asked.

I took in a deep breath and let it out. "Long enough to see how little you guys can act," I said.

They both looked at me and shrugged their shoulders. I sighed and walked out of the room. I went over to the front door and looked out into the dark sky. It looked so peaceful. But it didn't look like a peaceful night as far as Mandel was concerned.

Mandel was getting out of his limo that drove him to town. He walked over near an old warehouse. Then out of nowhere, someone grabbed his mouth and dragged him behind a van.

Mandel looked at the man who did this to him. There in front of him stood an exact replica of him. It was his brother. "Oh, what do you want now?" Mandel asked him.

M2 slugged him in the mouth. "Don't speak. I will do the talking. I understand that you didn't leave anyone at your house to watch over your little brats. Well, technically big brats."

M2 snapped his fingers and had a man come over and tie him up. "Take him to the place. I will go and get those kids."

The man looked at his boss, "But, sir, you two are wearing two very different things. Won't they know it's not you?"

M2 thought about what his help had told him. "You are right. Even though, it doesn't matter, I going to take them anyway. But you had a good point. Take off my brother's jacket. We will switch clothes."

The man did as he was told. M2 and his brother switched clothes.

M2 started to walk away into the limo his brother had taken. The man watched his master walk away then knocked out Mandel tied him up and gagged him. Then he put him in the van.

I was in the kitchen making an ice cream cone. I liked cookies and cream. I started to come out of the room when I bumped into Prinella. "Oh, excuse me, miss. But Sir Mandel is at the front door," she said.

I followed her to the door, and there stood Mandel just as she said. Then I remembered what Alistair told me—be careful.

Of course, I was going to be careful. Did he not think I was going to do that? Go up and give him a great big hug?

Before I spoke, I looked at him. At his eyes in particular. Mandel had soft eyes unlike his brother.

"You look surprised to see me," he said.

"Well, you said that you would be back late, like, in a couple of hours late. So yes, I am surprised to see you. Did you need something for you to be home so early?" I said.

He looked at me and gave a weird smile. "No, I wanted to tell you all something. So if you could go get Alistair and Carlos, that would be most appreciated."

I nodded and went to do what I was told. Alistair and Carlos were still in the game room, just sitting on the couch, talking. "Hey, guys, Mandel is back, and he would like to tell us all something."

Alistair gave me a strange look. "That's impossible, he won't be back until, like, eleven. And there's no way that he would just skip it (the meeting) and come back home unless someone's dying," he said.

I sighed. "Well, he's here, and he wants to tell us something."

Carlos looked at us then made his way slowly to the door. He peeked over at the man standing at the door who is supposed to be Mandel.

"It's not him," Carlos said.

I took in a deep breath. "How can you tell?" I asked.

"Our father doesn't have evil eyes this one does. Plus, he has Sketchers on and our father hates that brand," Carlos said to me.

Alistair pulled out the gun that he had in his shirt. "Okay, you two go out. If he asks for me, tell him that I had to finish up a game," he ordered.

Carlos and I nodded and went out. We walked out casually, talking about the video game they were playing. "You wanted to tell us something, Dad?" Carlos said, trying to sound sincere.

You could tell that M2 wasn't used to being called "Dad."
"Where's your brother?" he asked.

"Oh, don't worry about him. He's over there, finishing up his game," Carlos told him.

"Well, I don't wanna start without him so I will wait."

Carlos looked over at me. I nodded. "There's no need."

Then Carlos shoved his fist into M2's stomach. He staggered back but then came back at Carlos with energy. He punched Carlos in the eye. He was about to hit him again when Alistair came out of the other room. "Would you like to hit him again?" Alistair said while pointing his gun at M2.

M2 put his hand down and stared at Alistair. "What are you going to do?" M2 said. "Shoot me? I don't think so."

"Well, don't tempt me," Alistair answered back. "Natalie, Carlos, get back here."

M2 took in a deep breath. "So what are you going to do with me?"

"I don't know. But you're not going to get away with anything this time."

I always knew that Alistair was some kind of superhero. But this was kind of pathetic. It was like watching an old movie. And I hate old movies where the guy tries to be so cool then ends up losing.

M2 made a little chuckle that disturbed me. "What is it? Why are you laughing?" I asked him.

"Does anyone of you guys know where Mandel is? Is he at his meeting?" He started to laugh again that drove me crazy. I started to plunge toward him, screaming, "What did you do with him?"

Carlos and Alistair pulled me back. M2 didn't even move back but just kept laughing. "Wouldn't you like to know?"

"Yes, we would," Alistair agreed. "Now, are you going to tell us or do we need to help you tell us?"

M2 stopped and stared at Alistair. Both Alistair and M2's eyes were hollow and cold. "Yes, you do need to make him," he said bitterly.

Alistair took in a deep breath then slowly raised his gun. "Fine, you can't say that I didn't have the guts."

Carlos and I watched quietly. I didn't know what was going to happen. For all I knew, if Alistair pulled that trigger, all of our worries would be gone. But he just murdered someone who was unarmed.

Alistair held the gun pointing at his uncle for the longest time. Finally, he said, "You had your time to tell us. Now . . ."

He was interrupted by a voice behind us. "Put the gun down. Slowly turn around with your hands on your head."

I turned my head slightly to see who it was. I didn't recognize him. He had to have worked with M2. Speaking of him, he smiled. "Well, what are you going to do?" he asked Alistair.

Alistair didn't move when again the man said, "Put it down."

Soon, my boyfriend knelt to the ground, putting down his weapon. He turned around. We all did. M2 came up to stand next to his friend. Or his helper (he seemed to have a lot of those).

"Now, don't worry, I'll take you to your daddy," M2 said.

Between all of this, I only then realized how confusing and annoying it was to say "Mandel #2" all the time. So from here on out, I am going to address him as "M2."

M2 stared to come toward me. "Now you are coming with me."

Carlos and Alistair stepped in front of me. How nice it was to feel special. The man came up next to him with a gun. "You two guys better start walking," he said in a low tone of voice.

The man held the gun up to Carlos's head. "Move!" he said more loudly.

Finally, Carlos and Alistair started to move toward the door. Alistair grabbed my hand before he left.

"Oh, how cute," M2 mimicked. "But you do know that you three are going to go to the same place, right?"

M2 grabbed my arm and dragged me along outside with the rest of them. They were put in the limo. Soon, we were off to some place where hopefully Mandel was too.

While we were still in the house, I tried to understand why Prinella or one of the other maids came to help. Not that a maid would do anything to M2. But it would have been the thought that counted. Right?

We drove for about thirty minutes. M2 and his pal kept their guns pointed at us.

Soon we came to a stop. They took us out and hit us.

CHAPTER 18

Mandel woke up in a dark room. He was tied up with an abrade rope. Soon the lights flickered on. At first, he had to squint his eyes to see. When his vision came together, he could see M2 in front of him, smiling. "Well, my good brother, how are you?" he interrogated.

They were in an old beer warehouse.

Mandel just glared at him. "What do you want?" he asked ruthlessly.

M2's smile went from sarcastically cheerful one to a reluctant stare. "Oh, I don't know. Of course it wouldn't have anything to do with you giving my job to two non-coherent twerps," he said with sarcasm. (When he said "two non-coherent twerps," he was talking about my parents. Just to let you know.)

Mandel sighed. "You know why I did that? They were more professional than you were. They did a better job than you. And to be the head of the Mafia, the only thing to do was to knock you down and put them ahead of you."

"Yeah, whatever, I don't care anymore, I only have one question. How much do you love Natalie?"

Before M2 said that, Mandel's head was down. But then he looked up with desperate eyes. "Mark my words, if you do anything to that child, I will get you."

M2 made a little chuckle. "How? Do you mean, if I kill her like I did her parents?"

Mandel looked up. "You bastard. You're the who killed them!"

"Oh, please. Like you didn't know. Just answer the question."

When Mandel refused to answer, M2 hit him in the face. "It's a simple question, now answer it before you make me kill my own brother!"

Still Mandel was silent. M2 hit him three more times before he understood that he wasn't going to get anything from him anyhow.

That is unless he had the girl. "Just one moment my brother," M2 said.

He walked over to the door and called out, "Okay, bring them in."

When Mandel realized that his brother had Carlos, me, and Alistair. He struggled to get loose. And luckily, his brother wasn't very good at tying. So with a little pulling, he got it to a point to where he could get it undone. And when he did, he got up.

Two men came in pushing three teens—Carlos, me, and Alistair.

M2 turned around, knowing that his brother untied himself and pushed him in the face to make him sit back down.

Mandel brought his hand up to his mouth. And looked at us. I had a bloody nose, Alistair had redness around his face to where he was hit, and Carlos just had the same as mine.

"Now you might like to answer my question," M2 started to say.

He grabbed me, swung me over, and put his left arm up at my neck and tightened his grit. I looked at Mandel with scared eyes.

"Let her go," Mandel said.

"Well I just might, that is if you answer the question. Now how much do you like Natalie? I am willing to bargain her life for you two boys."

I started to cry. Not because I was scared but because his would tighten his grip every couple of minutes and it was making it very hard for me to breathe. "I care for her very much. She's almost like daughter. And for that, you will give me Carlos, Alistair, and Natalie."

M2 gave him a look that I'll never forget. "I am sorry, my brother, but that was not one of the choices so I will be forced to take all of them."

Then the two men came in again. One took my hand, and the other took Carlos and Alistair.

Then out of the corner of my eye, I saw M2 take Mandel forcefully and pulled out a gun.

"Before I kill you, my sweet brother, I will take you on a little field trip," M2 said.

"Hodgkins, bring the van around."

I didn't know what they were going to do to us. And preferably, I didn't think I would want to.

They took us outside. We walked, they pushed. I turned my head to look over at Carlos and Alistair. They had a hard face on. I then remembered what we learned from Yassen in boot camp: "Never show your enemy that you're scared."

And that was what I should be doing. I put that face on. And walked like Carlos and Alistair did.

Soon a big tan van came up. They pushed us in. Then M2 hopped in without Mandel. I was scared, and I didn't care if I showed it. We were going to die anyway. M2 pulled out a gun. (Don't ask me what kind.)

He pointed it at Mandel. "Good-bye, my brother."

Before Mandel could do anything, the gun made its shot and Mandel laid on the ground with blood on his leg.

Carlos and Alistair were still not doing anything. But their eyes got glassy. I knew that they wanted to cry. Alistair took in one deep breath. He was mad. Soon, people closed the door. The van started to move. I moved to look out of the window. I watched as Mandel slowly disappeared.

Soon I felt someone grab my shoulder and pull me back. "Stay away from that window," M2 ordered me.

I looked at him with harmful eyes and went over to sit with Alistair and Carlos. "Everything is going to be okay," Carlos comforted me as he put his arm around me.

"Oh, how cute," M2 said with a sarcastic tone.

Alistair got up and slammed his arm down on the side of the van. "I about had it. What do you want?" he spat.

M2 smiled. "You have a lot of nerve to say that to me."

"Why shouldn't I? At least if I wanted to kill someone, it would only take me one try. But with you, you failed at least two times. So why should I have nerve to talk to you? You're nothing but trash."

I looked over at Alistair with open eyes. I couldn't believe he said that. "Boy, my advice is for you to sit back down and shut up."

A man who was behind Alistair shoved him down on the seat. Soon I could feel us go around a sharp turn. We all went to one side of the van. I fell off the seat near the window. I took a quick glance out. We were on the highway.

I pulled myself away from the window. "Why are we on the highway?" I asked the evil twin.

He smiled. "Oh, my dear, I'm glad you asked," M2 said.

He made his way over to the door. He opened it. A burst of light came in. The three of us looked at each other. Cars were driving past us. Some looking in the van at us. "Who's first?" he asked.

"We need to talk about it," Carlos said.

The three of us formed sort of a group huddle. "Now this is what we are going to do. When I say so, we are going to take out those two guys and M2. Then we jump out of the van and run. Got it?" Carlos told us.

We both nodded. We got up and faced M2. "Alistair would like to go first," I said. Carlos and I stepped back.

"All right," the evil Mandel said. He grabbed Alistair's arm.

"Now," Carlos shouted.

At that time, I took one of the guys' arms and flipped him. (I was pretty proud of myself.) Carlos did the same thing. When we were done, we looked over at Alistair. M2 and he were at it. Finally, Alistair took him out with a rabbit punch. "Now jump," Carlos ordered.

At that moment, Carlos and Alistair jumped into the air. I was about to jump to when two hands grabbed onto my shoulders. I turned around. M2 slapped me. I fell down. I could hear Alistair and Carlos yelling at me.

CHAPTER 19

I was in the back of the van with my hands tied. I was drowsy from the night before but managed to stay awake. M2 was up front, talking to two other guys.

Soon one of them came over to me and pulled me up. He was big and ugly and had a bad odor, but that's not the point.

They were talking in a different language so I couldn't understand them. (My guess was it was Latin.) The big ugly guy started to push me. He then untied my hand and shoved me over to M2.

All three of them stared at me. M2 soon grabbed my arm. He gave me an evil smile. I didn't know what it meant at the time.

His tight grip numbed my arm. He dragged me over to the open door. His strong muscular arm tilted my head in an angle so I could get a good look at the pack of cars behind us.

Then he pulled me back in. He gave an evil smile at me again. I soon figured out what he was going to do. He was going to push me off the van.

M2 opened the van door more. Soon enough he looked at me. He put his two hands on my shoulders.

Then without a doubt, he grabbed my neck and pulled me back. He was getting ready to shove me out of the vehicle.

Like any girl, I was not just going to stand there and wait to die. I grabbed his arm and flipped him. I got him off my back for a few minutes.

After he got up, I only realized that I should not have done that. A rush of steam ran through his veins. He stomped over to me. I had my mercy/pity-me face on. All I can say is that it was a tough crowd. It didn't work. But then in the past few months, he was trying to kill me. And I don't think a little cute face was going to change his mind.

He grabbed my arm but tightened the grip even more. I winced. I tried to get away, but it didn't help. Again, he pulled me back, and then out of the blue, he forced me forward.

I lost my balance and flew into the air. I tumbled onto the ground. I looked back. I saw Alistair and Carlos running up to me. They were about ten feet away from me. I looked back at the van. He was coming back for me. M2 knew that I wasn't dead yet.

The van was about to come past me. M2 was facing me with his gun. I knew that this was the end. I looked back at the guys one more time. Carlos was in front of Alistair.

I then turned to face the van that was about to do a drive-by on me. M2's gun faced me. I closed my eyes. I couldn't bear to watch myself die. Even though I would be dead before I could think about how it felt.

My eyes were closed. And while they were closed, I was thinking about everything that I did in my short life. Then I heard a shot go off. At first I thought that I was dead because I couldn't feel anything. But when I opened my eyes, I saw Carlos on the ground with a blotch of blood on his chest.

I screamed, "Carlos."

I then looked up at the van; it was driving away. A *boom* came from the van. It was up in flames. Since it was going the opposite of the other cars, it ran into one. I made a quick smile at it then turned to Carlos.

I knelt down on the ground. I put his head down on my knees. Alistair soon joined us. "I'll call an ambulance," he said.

"I thought you don't trust them," I replied.

Alistair stopped in his tracks. "We don't, but in this case, we have to."

With Alistair off getting help, I was to stay there by myself with Carlos. I could feel his big heart beat faster and faster. His breathing became heavy.

"I'm sorry," he told me.

I took a deep breath, trying to hold back the tears. "What do you mean? You saved my life. I should be the one to say sorry"

He smiled. His breathing started to become heavy again. "Just relax, the ambulance is on its way."

He shook his head. "No."

I looked at him. I looked at his eyes. They were full of love. He wasn't sad or scared about dying. He didn't care that his life was about to end. Or maybe he didn't get it.

"I don't want to live. And saving your life and ending mine were the way to go. I should never had done what I did to you."

I had to think. What did he ever do to me?

I didn't know what I was to say. "What do you mean? You never hurt me."

"I told Father that since you parents died, you should come to live with us. I told him that you would love to join the Mafia. And look where it got you. People tried to kill you, and everything is my fault. Do you understand?"

"No, I don't. Being here with you guys was one of the best things that happened to me."

He coughed and blood came out. His arm came up and touched my hand. "There's one more thing." He slowly pulled a piece of paper out of his shirt. He put it in my hand.

I nodded. "Yassen . . ." He took a deep breath. I watched his stomach go down as he exhaled. Then his eyes slowly closed. His face became pale. He was dead.

I couldn't stop it this time. Tears arose from my eyes. I brought my eyes up to my face. I looked down the roads. Everything as blurry with my tears. No one seemed to stop and ask if everything was okay. They just kept going past.

I sat there in the middle of the grass that separated the different directions of the roads, with Carlos on my lap.

About fifteen minutes later, an ambulance came up and stopped near us. Alistair got out. "Sorry, it took so long. We stopped to pick up father on the way," he informed.

I wiped away my eyes. "I am too," I said while looking down at Carlos.

Alistair looked down at him. "No!" he screamed. He half-ran about five feet away. He let himself drop to his knees.

The paramedics brought a body bag over. They helped me up and asked me if I was okay.

I watched as they put Carlos's body into a big black plastic bag. Then they placed it into the vehicle.

I walked over to Alistair. I put my hand on his shoulder. Every time that I needed him, he was there. Now it was time for me to be there for him. "Are you okay?" I asked him.

When he didn't answer, I knelt down like he did. "Everything will be all right," I comforted him.

He shook his head. "Nope, my brother's dead because of my hateful uncle, and my father is in critical condition. I hardly have a family now. Nothing will be all right after this."

I sighed. "I'm sorry to hear that. I'm sorry but I need to go now. I can't stay here any longer. I'll meet you over at the hospital to see how your father's doing."

I got up and patted Alistair's shoulder. "I'll be at the house."

I turned to leave when Alistair said, "Wait, I'll come too."

I nodded but continued to walk. "Natalie," Alistair said, "I'm sorry for what I said. I didn't mean it. You're part of our family. I just meant like it would just be the three of us if Father makes it."

I smiled. "I know."

We then took hands and walked toward the limo that awaited us. The paramedics came up to us and said that they would like if we went into the hospital later to make sure that we had all of the information correct.

CHAPTER 20

The ride home was silent. We didn't even sit next to each other. With only two people, the limo seemed bigger than normal. Hopefully, there would be three soon.

When we got there, it wasn't "Finally we're home" kind of feelings. It was more "Okay, now what?" type. It was as if we were happy that we were home, but we didn't want to be home.

I walked in before Alistair did. He was still in the car. I opened the door to the house. For to me, it was no longer a home. Well, for now, it wasn't.

When I opened the door, there was an echo. I pulled the piece of paper that Carlos gave me out of my pocket. I wanted to read it but couldn't. I went into his room and laid it on his night stand.

Then I headed for my room. My bed was made, and my maids were putting up new curtains. "Oh, we'll be out of your way in just a minute," said Prinella.

"Oh, no, take as much time as you need," I insisted.

They smiled as they got down off the ladder. "Well, then, if you say so, then we will go ahead and put the other one up."

I nodded while I then decided to go and get a book to read from the study. I walked down the stairs, slowly and contently.

Downstairs was quiet. You could probably hear a pin drop. I turned left to go to the study. However, in order to get there, you have to pass the game room. When I walked past it, I peeked in. There on the sofa sat Alistair, watching TV. "Here on this very highway died two Mafia personnel. Carlos Mandel and Lar Mandel #2. The people who were driving while this tragic scene was going on said that Lar Mandel #2 pushed Miss Natalie out of a van. Then tried to shot her when Carlos stepped in front of her. He gave his own life to help his friend. Also, Lar Mandel, the present Mafian ruler, was shot in the leg by his own brother and is in the hospital in critical condition," said the TV.

Well, the TV didn't exactly say it, the news lady Jenna Levine did.

I walked into the room. "May I sit down?" I asked him.

He nodded. "Yeah, sure, why not? It's not like there's anyone else who will," he answered.

So I sat down. "I'm sorry," I told him.

He looked at the TV then turned his attention toward me. "What do you mean you're sorry?"

"I'm sorry that Carlos died. I can't imagine the pain that you're going through right now. It must be dreadful."

"Yeah, but you had to watch him die. You held him in his arms until he took his last breath. You must be pretty shook up about that."

"Yeah, but he was your brother, and that must really hurt. And I know that I'll never be able to fill in the gap that is now in your heart." I left it at that and got up from the seat. "I'll be in the study."

He nodded and watched me go out. "Why don't you stay awake? We could watch TV."

I thought about it for a while then walked over and plopped down next to him. "Did you hear what they said about us?" Alistair asked while motioning toward the TV with his head.

"Yep, I was listening in while I was walking past the room. How did they find out about that?" I asked.

"They have geeks who, like, spy on us looking for any news material."

"Yeah, but how did they know that we would be on the highway? Do they, like, just roam around spying on us?"

Alistair scratched his head. "Yeah, that's about the size of that."

"Isn't that illegal?"

"I don't know. News reporters will do anything to get a good story these days."

"So normally you don't, like, have any privacy?"

"Oh, we get privacy. The public is sort of scared of us. But hey, I can't blame them. And if you be nice to them, they think that you're playing with their minds to brainwash them and kill 'em."

I nodded understandingly. "So what's on?"

He shrugged while flipping through the channels. "Do you wanna watch *Clifford*? I think Emily Elizabeth is hot."

I looked over at him. "You are pathetic."

I started to get up and leave. "I was kidding," he said while laughing.

Knowing he was kidding, I laughed as well. I walked out of the room and headed for my original objective—to get a book to read from the study.

My smile faded. I then remembered a movie I once saw. About how someone was like a stance of silence because of a death. Knowing I didn't want that to happen to me, I had to try to keep cool. Then later I'll bring out all my tears.

I flickered on the light when the phone rang. "I got it," I said to Alistair as he headed back to the game or hang out room to get it. "Hello," I answered.

There was a slight pause. "Um, yes hello. Is *Miss* Natalie or Sir Alistair available?" the person on the line asked.

"Um, Miss Natalie speaking. May I ask who is calling?"

"Oh, yes, my name is Dr. Patrick Sholes. I am from the hospital Sir Lar Mandel is."

I shifted my eyes. I peeked over at Alistair, who was looking at me. "Yes, um, is Mandel okay. How is he doing?"

There was another pause. The doctor made a slight sigh. "I'm afraid to inform you that he is not doing very well. He lost a lot of blood. And is in shock. We were wondering if you and Sir Alistair would have time to come down to the hospital to answer a few questions?"

"Yes, yes, we'll be on our way right now. Good-bye."

I hung up the phone before the doctor could say good-bye or anything else.

I noticed that Alistair was still looking at me. "Mandel's not doing good. Doc wants us to go there to answer some questions," I told him.

He turned off the TV and raced up to catch me.

"Prinella, have the driver pull up at the front door," Alistair ordered.

The maid nodded and ran off.

We waited about five minutes for the limo to pull up. Then without even waiting for the driver to come over and open the door, we just crawled in. "To the hospital. And be quick about it," Alistair ordered once again.

It was quiet once again as we drove to the hospital. I don't know if it was the tension, despondence, curiosity, worry, or resentment about what happened earlier. But whatever it was, it was heavily on our minds.

I don't know if it was on Alistair's mind at the time, but I was eager to find out what questions he wanted to ask us. What if it was about funeral arrangements if Mandel would die? So many possibilities.

We drove up to the front of the hospital. We went in. The lady at the front desk said to go on the elevator, second level, and go to the left for room 209.

We went to room 209, but the door was closed. We knocked, and then we heard, "Oh, good you're here" from behind us. We turned around and Dr. Sholes was standing with his hands in front of him.

He was a middle-aged man. About in his thirties. Brown hair. With a white jacket on with a black tie and black pants. He looked very professional, but his face was hard and robust that he had no intention of making this an enjoyable meeting.

"Yes, now you said that you had some questions for us," Alistair said in a controlling manner.

"Ah, yes, please follow me."

He walked out in front of us. "Now remember, public hospitals don't particularly like us so don't be too nice to him and don't trust him," Alistair reminded me.

I nodded and headed into the room that Dr. Sholes pointed to. It was a nice room. My guess was that it was a place where the immediate family and the doctors come to talk about their patient, just as we were doing.

He offered us to sit down. We sat down directly across from his and put our hands on the table in front of us. "Now, over the phone you informed us that my father wasn't doing very well. Would you like to tell us about that?" Alistair said again in a very controlling power of speech.

I could tell that he was going to be the one talking most of the time.

The doctor smiled as if amused with how Alistair was acting toward him. "I don't think this is funny," Alistair said straight at him.

"Neither do I. Now, your father has been hit in the nerve of his leg. As he lost a lot of blood. Now there is a good chance that he might regain his sense of feel again, that is if he makes it," Dr. Sholes said.

I sighed, "Okay, and what can you do to help him?"

"Um, are you part of the immediate family?" the doctor asked.

Alistair rolled his eyes. "Look, Dr. Sholes, this is all you have to work with. Now she is going to be immediate family that you will deal with. I might be a teenager, but I have to power to put you out of business permanently so I suggest you cooperate and not worry about how we are related to Mandel. Do I make myself clear? Now answer Miss Natalie," Alistair said, starting to get agitated.

I looked over at him, I couldn't believe that I just heard that come out of his mouth. In all the months, years, or however long you want to call it, I have never heard him act like this.

Dr. Sholes cleared his throat. "Yes, sir. Um, we are doing all we can. Unfortunately, he isn't responding to the medicine that we affording him. Do I answer your question?"

Alistair looked at me. "Yes, thank you, that is all I wanted to know," I said.

The man nodded. I was quite sure he was embarrassed by getting told by a teenager. But who could blame him? I would be too.

"Now, about funeral arrangements," he said shortly after.

We both looked at the doctor. "Let's face it, the bullet hit him at close range. And it hit his nerve, he lost a great amount of blood, and he isn't responding to any of the medicines. Now let's say we're talking about another person, but the same symptoms are occurring. Do you think he or she would make it?" the doctor asked in explanation.

I had to think. Maybe he did make a little sense, but his attitude was currently unacceptable. "I don't care if it's someone else. I would think you should try to help whoever is in need of your assistance. Don't you think?" I said, speaking my mind. Even though I didn't really think I made much sense.

"Yes, we do help people, but when it comes to your kind of people, how do we know that you not in here to blow us up," Dr. Sholes analyzed who was looking over at Alistair.

His last statement made Alistair get up. "That's it, we are out of here. And we are going to take Mandel with us."

I got up as Dr. Sholes did. "You don't have the jurisdiction to do that," he said, thinking he was going to outsmart Alistair this time.

Alistair sighed. "Sir, I think if you have the heart to be this cold, then I have the jurisdiction of any adult. Now, if you would be so kind as to get the papers that *we* need to sign I think you should get them *now*."

Once again, Dr. Sholes had the look of defeat. "I don't like you."

Alistair smiled. "I don't think it matters if you like me or not."

Dr. Sholes walked over to the filing cabinet and picked out two yellow papers. "Here, give them to me at the front desk when you are ready."

"Thank you," I said as I took them from him.

I sat down with Alistair to fill them out. "You were great," I told him.

He smiled. "I was, wasn't I?"

We both gave a little chuckle then sat ourselves down to answer the questions in order to get Mandel out of this junky place. (No offense to the people who like the hospitals. Just that if you're part of the Mafia, you don't really get along with people.)

My face turned serious again. I looked over at Alistair who was trying not to notice. "Speaking of funeral arrangement—"

"Yeah, I know," Alistair said, interrupting me.

"So where do you want it to be at?"

He sighed. "I don't know. But let's get these papers ready so we don't have another funeral to prepare."

I nodded and read and signed the papers needed. When we were done, we went out to the front desk as Dr. Sholes asked us to.

We stood there for long enough to understand that this was shady. In other words, pathetic. I looked behind the desk. No one was out. "Maybe he's in Mandel's room," I suggested.

We looked at each other. I hurried to Mandel's room. It had a "Do Not Enter" sign on it. We didn't even bother to obey it. We walked right into the room. There we saw Dr. Sholes putting something in Mandel's IV.

"What are you doing in here?" he asked while putting a bottle of liquid in his pocket.

"Might we ask you the same question?" I asked.

"I am his doctor. I am allowed."

"Not anymore now. If you touch him again, then you will be in deep trouble," Alistair said.

We gave him the papers that he asked for. He looked over them and sighed. "Well, looks like he's yours. Now take that piece of trash out of my hospital before he wakes up and kills someone," the doctor said.

I looked at him. Alistair smiled. He walked over put his hand on Dr. Sholes's shoulder. He smiled again but then slammed his fist into the doctor's stomach.

Dr. Sholes bent over to hold his stomach. Then Alistair started to walk out of the room. I watched him then hurried to go over by his side. We were about to go out of the room when Dr. Sholes started to get up.

Once again, Dr. Sholes had the look of defeat. "Don't think that I won't remember this night," the doctor said, almost as a threat.

Alistair smiled. "And don't think we won't be ready."

Then we waited for him to go out of the room before we did the same. We couldn't move Mandel until we got someone over here to transfer him so we decided to let him in peace until it was time (if you know what I mean.)

We stayed in that one meeting room that we did earlier. We were standing over at the far end of the room. Alistair was standing over at the window. "What are you thinking about?" I asked him.

His eyes were glassy. His expression didn't make sense. He blinked a couple of times as if he was dazing out. "W-what?" he stuttered.

I sighed. "What are you thinking about? Are you okay?"

He took in a deep breath and came away from the window. "I'm just thinking about what I'll do about Carlos's funeral. We have to get started with that soon."

I nodded. "Yeah, and the sad thing is that Mandel doesn't even know about his son's death. And he won't be able to go to his funeral."

"Yeah."

He put his left hand in his pocket. Then he turned to look at me. He shook his finger at me. "Maybe we can get him to the funeral."

I didn't understand. "Oh, boy, what do you mean?"

"Well, it's not like he's in a coma. Well, maybe there's something that we can give him to get him going."

I shook my head in disagreement. "Dr. Sholes was giving him medication. And you heard him as well as I did. Mandel isn't reacting to the stuff. It's hopeless. It's going to take a miracle."

He made a depressed expression. "Yeah, well, maybe you're right."

There was a long silence when my cell phone rang. I flipped it open and answered, "Hello."

"Yes, this is Dr. Hampton, Miss Natalie. I heard that you and Alistair have called," the other line said.

I put my hand up to the part to where you speak into and looked over at Alistair. "It's Dr. Hampton," I told him.

He nodded and put his hand out to have the phone. Without knowing any better, I gave it to him.

"Hello, sir," Alistair said to Dr. Hampton. "Yes, it is good to talk to you as well. Um, I do hope you got my message. Yes, oh, good thank you, we will have him out in fifteen minutes. Yes, right, I'll remember, good. Bye-bye."

I was looking at him. "What did the doctor say? Are you going to pick up Mandel? Well, what did he say?" I asked anxiously.

He gave me back my cell. "Oh, he'll be over in about fifteen twenty minutes. And he said that it was good to hear your voice again," he explained to me.

I gave an understanding nod and got up from the seat I was sitting on. "I'll go and tell the nurses to get Mandel ready to go," I said.

CHAPTER 21

An ambulance was outside the hospital in about ten minutes. By the time Dr. Hampton made his way up to Mandel's room, we were waiting for him. He nodded at us. "It's good to see you again, Miss Natalie," he said as he walked toward me.

I found that even though he wasn't going to be doing any examinations, doctors always seem to need that black bag with them.

I smiled. "Please, call me Natalie." I hate formality.

He smiled as he brought my hand up to kiss it. Once he put it down, he turned toward Alistair. "It's good to see you too, sir."

Alistair nodded and put his hand out to shake Dr. Hampton's. "Likewise."

"So what is this about wanting to transfer Mandel? Would you like to fill me in on this?"

Alistair nodded. "Yes, well, if you join us, we can fill you in on everything."

Dr. Hampton agreed, and we showed him to the room. We all sat down at the table. "So tell me, what's going on?"

Alistair took in a deep breath. "Well, to cut it short, Mandel had to go to one of his meetings as he does. But as he was gone, M2 came dressing just like him. But we knew it wasn't him (Mandel) so we got the drop on him but he overcomes us. Then he takes us to Mandel where he captured him, sort of. Then he shoots Mandel in the leg and takes us away on the highway where he shoves Carlos and me out of a van. Soon enough he shoves Natalie off. Then he turned the van around to come after Natalie to shoot her, but Carlos gets in the way. And now he's dead. And M2 got blown up," Alistair said in one big breath.

Dr. Hampton sat there, looking at us. "Well, I guess you had a busy late few days. And sorry for Carlos. He as a good lad. Now about Mandel. You wanna take him back home? How do you plan to do that?"

I took in a deep breath. To tell you the truth, all I really wanted to do was go home and take a hot bath. And leave Alistair here to take care of all this. But I didn't. I stared at Dr. Hampton. He was nodding to everything that Alistair was saying. Then my eyes turned to him. Alistair's hands lay on the table. He had a professional expression on his face. It kind of scared me a little.

Alistair cleared his throat. "Well, sir, we were going to ask you if you would like to take care of Mandel until he is well again. We are ready to pay you very well in order for you to do this."

Dr. Hampton did say a word. "Really?" He looked over at me.

I nodded in a serious manor.

"Well. Mandel and I are close friends. I would like it very much to come and help you guys. And please, don't pay me. It would make me feel bad. Agreed?"

Alistair and I looked at each other. "Yes, and thank you, sir," Alistair said.

"Now, shall we go and take your father home?"

Alistair and I both nodded.

We got up, pushed in our chairs, and headed out the door and went over to the nurses' station to tell them to get Mandel ready for transportation. "Okay, I'll stay here with him while you two go home and get everything ready for you father," Dr. Hampton said.

Alistair and I nodded, and we headed down the hall to the elevator. "Aren't you glad that Mandel is coming home?" he asked me.

I looked over at him. There was a light in his eye. He couldn't wait for his family to be back in his house again. I looked away, and because of me, he wouldn't have his whole family.

I shrugged. He looked at me in disbelief. "You're not happy for him to be home?"

"I never said that. But no matter who comes home, it won't feel like home."

He nodded. "Yeah, and Yassen won't be home for another month or three weeks."

"Yeah, I wonder what he's doing."

Alistair didn't say anything. We stood there in silence. The door to the elevator opened, and two gentleman walked out. They gave a faint smile and nodded. "Sir," one said to Alistair.

Alistair nodded back and waited for me walk into the small room before him. He stepped in after and pushed the button that said ground one. "Do they know you?" I asked with curiosity in my voice.

Alistair shrugged. "I don't know them, but at least they know how to show respect. People nowadays don't know how to show respect to people who are younger than them.

I looked at him. "So people normally call you *sir*? Why don't they call me anything? This is shady."

He looked at me obscurely. "*Shady?*"

I looked at him innocently. "Hey, I read it in a book."

He took in a deep breath. "We really need to teach you how to use a bigger vocabulary. And as far as not giving you respect, they do."

I looked at him openly. "Yeah, right. As much as we want to believe that, we both know that it's not going to happen."

He looked at me with open eyes and sighed. "Yeah, I guess you're right. But hey, you're just perfect without a big vocab."

I rolled my eyes. "Oh thanks."

He smiled and put his arm about my shoulders. The door opened to the elevator, and people were standing there. They saw us and stepped out of our way. "Miss," one of the ladies said.

I smiled and nodded. "Good day," another person said to me.

I didn't even bother looking over at Alistair. I could tell that he was, well, he wasn't very happy.

We made it out of the building. I started to laugh. Alistair stopped and looked at me. I kept walking but looked back at him. "Ha-ha no one said anything to you. What happened to their respect?"

He looked at me and raised an eyebrow then he started to run toward me. I screamed and started to run. He ran up to tickle me. I laughed and ran over into the limo. The people outside just looked at us and smiled. *It's good to see young people have a good time* was what they probably thought.

We drove home talking about things. Things that you don't need to know. You get it right—personal things.

The driver helped me out when we got home. When we got inside, we saw a whole bunch of maids and people moving things around. "What is going on?" Alistair asked.

Everyone stopped and went silent. They all looked over at Alistair. The way their faces looked. They stared at him as if he was the man of the house, eager to please him.

Alistair paused, surprised to see them stop at his command. "Um, what is this all about?" he said, softening his voice.

Prinella stood there. "Dr. Hampton phoned us about the news with Sir Mandel coming home and told us to get the house ready," she explained to us.

I nodded. "Oh, well, thank you, but the house looks wonderful and you have the rest of the day off," I assured them.

They nodded with pleasure and walked away. Alistair turned to me. "The rest of the day off? Are you crazy? Who's going to make us dinner?"

I looked at him. This was sad. "Are you serious? You can't handle making dinner for one night? That is pitiful."

Alistair looked at me, unwilling. "Look, babe, I don't cook. So it's up to you."

I stared at him. He was so full of surprises. First he asks me out, doesn't talk me, then talks to me, kisses me, now he's calling me "babe." Sorry, I have a habit to think to myself.

"Fine, I have no problem cooking as long as you don't mind eating toasted cheese."

He looked at me. "What's that?"

My mouth dropped open. Was he serious? Then he smiled. I knew he was kidding. I took my hand and smacked him. "You're bad." I said, smiling.

We both smiled then. Soon, we heard the doorbell ring. Alistair looked at me. "Let's hope it's them."

I walked over to open the door. There stood the doctor. "Are you ready?" he asked us.

"For what?" Alistair asked.

Dr. Hampton looked at Alistair. "For you father to come inside."
"Oh yes."

Dr. Hampton nodded, assuring him. Alistair put his crossed arms in front of him. I thought about doing that, but I didn't. I just stood there with my hands in my pockets.

The paramedics people carried Mandel inside on a stretcher thing. They followed us up the stairs to his room. We opened the door for them, and they did the rest. In thirty minutes, everything was done.

Dr. Hampton came out of the room and said, "You may go in a see him now."

We walked in and saw him lying there, still and quiet. "How is he? Do you know when he's going to wake up?" I asked, concerned.

The doctor shook his head. "I don't know, Natalie. Even though it's only a shot to the leg, it can give some pretty bad side effects. Especially since it was at close range."

I nodded understandingly. I looked down at my feet. "I guess we'll just go and let him rest," Alistair said while taking my hand.

"How about you two go on a walk around the pond?" Dr. Hampton suggested.

I shrugged. "Okay," I agreed.

Alistair opened the door for me to go out. "Hang on," Alistair said. "I wanna talk to the doctor for a second."

I nodded. "I'll be downstairs," I said. I walked down.

Dr. Hampton looked at Alistair. "He's not good," Dr. Hampton said.

Alistair nodded and took in a deep breath. "How bad?" Alistair asked in a low pitch.

"It's hard to say, but normally if someone got hit, they would at least be up."

Alistair kept on doing nothing but nod. "Don't worry, I'll take care of him, you go off with Natalie," the doctor assured his friend.

Alistair turned to go downstairs.

I was downstairs waiting for Alistair to come down. Finally I saw him and started to make my way outside. He caught up with me. He fell into step with me. It was very silent for the first few minutes. Then he said, "So what you wanna talk about?"

I shrugged even though I knew he didn't see me. "I don't know. What did you say to Dr. Hampton? Or can't I know?"

Alistair picked up a pebble and threw it out in front of us. We took the long path down by the pond. The sun started to go down, and it was reflecting off the water. It was actually very pretty.

"Oh, nothing, just about how my father was doing."

"Isn't he doing very good?"

"Oh, yes of course. I was just asking about when he think he'll be able to walk."

"Oh, um, okay. So why are we actually out here?"

Alistair walked out in front to look at the swans swimming in the pond. I walked over there as well. "I don't really know why, but the doctor said for us to so I guess here we are."

"So you didn't have any special reason to be out here?"

"No, not really. Why?"

"Because I was going to go in and watch some TV. You wanna join me?"

Alistair stood there, staring at the pond. I put my hand in front of him and waved it a little. He didn't blink. I took my fingers and snapped. Still no response. Then finally he drew his head back. "What? Um, no thanks. I'm going to stay here and think. I'll be in soon."

I sighed. I started to walk away. He grabbed my hand and pulled me toward him. Then, like, poof, we were kissing. Finally, and I mean finally, we drew apart. Well, I shouldn't say *drew*. It doesn't sound right.

Finally, when it ended, he looked at me and said, "Sorry." Nothing else but sorry. I looked at him and smiled.

Then, once again, I turned to go back inside. I did what I said I was going to do. I went up to my room and watched TV.

CHAPTER 22

I got up and walked over to the window. The was a limo waiting for something. Then I remembered about the funeral.

Wait, rewind. I missed a couple of days. All that happened was Alistair and I didn't really talk and the house was pretty much quiet.

A knock came from the door. "Come in," I said, without looking to see who it was. I was still looking out.

"Miss, you're supposed to be ready," the person said.

I turned around to see Prinella standing there, looking at me. She was sad too.

"Oh, I'm sorry. I'll get dressed right away. What time were we going to be leaving?" I asked.

"Oh, please don't be sorry. And they were going to be leaving in about thirty minutes."

"Thank you."

She left the room. I didn't know what I was going to wear. Then I remembered that I had an outfit picked out since yesterday.

I walked over to the chair. I had a black skirt and a black shirt. I quickly put it on and did my hair. Then I had to put on those nylon things. You know, the things that girl put on before their shoes. I hate those things.

I'm all ready and headed downstairs. There I saw Alistair standing at the bottom of the staircase. He had his hands in front of him. He didn't look very happy. How could he? We were about to go to his brother's funeral.

I was still sad that Mandel couldn't come. It was his son, for heaven's sake. I came to the last couple of stairs. Alistair looked at me and held out his hand.

While looking at him, I took it. I didn't really know why we had to get all dressed up. I mean, the burial place was right outside the door over at the big oak tree. Alistair and I walked out the door.

I looked behind me as all of the maids followed us. When we got outside, I saw Dr. Hampton there. He waved as he walked toward us. "Natalie, I'm so sorry," he said.

He stretched out his hands to give me a hug. I let go Alistair's hand and walked over to give Dr. Hampton a hug. Then I rejoined Alistair's hand.

The three of us walked over to the tree. There we saw a preacher and two men standing next to the casket. I looked down as I saw the box-shaped object. There inside laid my best friend.

Soon as we were over at the tree, the preacher started to speak. "Today is a day of—"

To be honest, I didn't really listen to him. I never liked funerals. Especially since Carlos was the one who died. I stared at the hole that was going to hold my friend for the years to come.

I felt tears start to roll down my face as the preacher ended his prayer and the two men started to put the box in the ground.

I looked down at my feet. I felt Alistair's hand come around my shoulder. I leaned into his shoulder. I was crying. I practiced how I was going to act for the last few days. And after all of the replaying I did in my mind, I couldn't help the tears from coming.

I didn't watch for the rest of the funeral. I just closed my eyes and cried. Finally when everything was over and everyone was inside talking, I walked over to the tombstone. I knelt down and put two roses. "I'm sorry," I said.

I pulled out a tissue and dabbed my eyes.

I stood up and turned to walk back inside. Today was dreary. And I don't mean because today was the funeral. I looked up in the sky, it was gray, and I heard thunder. I could feel drops of rainfall onto my shoulders.

I started to run into the house. Right when I reached the door to go in, it started pouring. I opened it and closed it behind me. The house like echoed as the rain came down on the roof.

It was so quiet. I didn't know what to do. I went into the game room and sat down on the sofa. I just closed my eyes and thought, *What was I to do now?*

Soon Alistair joined me. He took my hand and pulled me up from the couch. Then he sat down and pulled me down on his lap. He held me tight (I just looked down). I didn't even care about anything.

"It will be okay," he said.

I didn't say anything. "I know it will," I said at last.

"You better get some sleep."

I nodded. I got up off of his lap and head out of the room. I walked slowly to my room. When I opened the door, I turned on the lights. Without even thinking about changing into my nightwear. I just went to bed. Even though it was only four in the afternoon. I fell asleep in a flash.

CHAPTER 23

I was in the study, trying to think about the book I was reading. But putting in little effort to do so, I wasn't getting very far. I closed the book and slammed it on the desk. I couldn't help think about the funeral yesterday and how Mandel couldn't be there.

I got up and walked over to the many shelves of books. I put back the one I got out and took out another. I put my pointer finger up to the titles and skimmed across the books, hoping to find a book I could keep an interest in after the first page.

Finally, I gave up and plopped down on the chair and closed my eyes. Everything was dark. And I'm not saying that just because my eyes were closed. The atmosphere was so quiet, alone, dark. With Mandel being upstairs in bed, trying to recuperate and Carlos gone. If felt strange to be in this house.

A knock on the door brought me to open my eyes. In the doorway stood Alistair. He looked at me with soft and understanding eye. He too didn't know what to do. "Wanna take a walk?" he asked.

I breathed in, looked at the bookshelves, and nodded.

I got up and walked over in his direction. He took my hand, and I followed him outside. It was sunny and warm. I looked over in the direction of the oak tree. Alistair saw what I was looking at and pulled me in that direction.

We walked over to the tree. I looked down at the ground. I turned and looked at Alistair. He looked straight ahead. I started to walk away.

"I know it's hard for you," he said as he took my hand and we walked down a different path.

I shrugged. "Sure," I told him.

Alistair sighed. I could tell he didn't know what to say to me. "Yassen will be gone for the next couple of weeks, maybe even month. And the way my father is, it's only making the house gloomy. So I arranged for a jet—"

"Are you going somewhere?" I stopped him.

He took in a deep breath. "As I was saying, I arranged for a private jet. I talked to some people about it, and I have planned for *us* to go to Tahiti in two days. That is, if you wanna go."

I looked at him. Was he crazy? Of course I would want to go. It's Tahiti he's talking about. "Yeah sure, I'll go," I replied nicely and calmly.

He nodded. "Oh, well then, I'd like to just go and talk to some people about it."

I shook my head yes. I watched him as he went inside. I was going to Tahiti. Just imagining it made a smile appear on my face. I decided to go in and think about what all I was going to bring. After all, we were leaving in two days.

I walked back into the house. As I passed the oak tree, I slowed down. Soon I stopped in front of it. I smiled. *I'm going to Tahiti,* I thought to him. *I wish you could come with me.*

I then walked back inside. I headed up to my room. I opened the door and went over to my storage closet and pulled out suitcases. Then I went into my clothes closet. I walked in and sat down on a small seat nearby. I looked around at all of my clothes. *What to wear, what to wear,* I thought.

Then I looked over at a drawer. It had "Swim Suits" printed on it. I smiled and walked over to it. I pulled it open. I picked out two bikinis. I brought them over and put them in a bag along with a beach towel.

Then I went over and pick out different pairs of flip-flops. I packed those as well. After that, I put in random pairs of shorts and tank tops.

After I was done, I went over to my bed and turned on the TV. I put on the weather channel to see how warm it was going to be.

"For the next two weeks, it will be sunny and warm high of ninety-five degrees Fahrenheit," the man on the TV said.

He walked from one end to the other on the TV. I just stared at it bored. Then I heard a knock on the door. It opened and in walked Prinella. "I thought you would like a glass of ice tea," she said as she brought in a tray.

I smiled and sat up. "Sure, just as long as you sit down and have one with me," I told her.

Her face turned red. "Oh, I don't know miss . . ."

I shook my head. "No, you're not busy, you can stand to have an ice tea with me," I insisted.

She shrugged her shoulders and brought over my ice tea. Then she walked over to her tray that she put on the coffee table. She sat down on the seat and poured herself a glass.

I shook my head. I got off my bed and walked over to sit down next to her. As I sat down on the seat beside her, she stood up. I sighed. "You can sit down, Prinella."

She slowly sat back down. It was clear that she wasn't used to sitting with one of her "bosses," so to speak.

I took a sip from my glass. "So Prinella, how old are you, if I may ask?"

"Nineteen, miss. I'll be twenty in two months."

I nodded. She looked over at me. "Miss, may I ask you something?"

"As long as you call me Natalie," I told her.

"No, miss. I couldn't."

I nodded. "When we are in my room, you may talk to me as your friend."

She sighed and looked at me hesitantly. "Okay, Natalie, what is it like to kiss someone?"

I put my glass down. "You mean you never kissed someone?"

Her face reddened with embarrassment. "No, miss."

I smiled. "Well, if you didn't kiss yet, that just means that you haven't found the right guy. That's all."

A smile spread across her face. "Thank you, miss. Well, I better be going. Maybe we can talk again too."

I nodded as she got up and headed to the door. "Bye, Prinella," I said.

She stopped. "Bye, Natalie."

When she left the room, I smiled to myself. Then the door opened, and in came Alistair. He looked at his watch. "It's five. You wanna go get a bite to eat in town?" he asked me.

I smiled. "Sure."

I went over and grabbed my sweatshirt. I took his hand, and we left the house. We went outside into the driveway. "Aren't we going to take a car?" I asked, pointing to the shed that the limos were in.

Alistair shook his head. "No, it's nice out, I thought we could walk," he said.

I nodded my head. "Okay, that works."

We walked for an hours until we got into town. We went into a restaurant. We sat down and ordered. "So are you all ready to go?" Alistair asked me.

"For what?" I asked.

"To go to Tahiti. I was wondering if you would like to go tomorrow instead?"

I shrugged. "Okay, that works."

For three hours, we were there, talking about our past. We laughed and ate.

We didn't come home until, like, one in the morning.

I woke up around nine. Soon the door flung open. I quickly covered myself with the covers. (I didn't want just anyone seeing me in my PJs.)

When it was only Alistair, I relaxed. "You need to get ready. We're heading off in one hour. You need to get dressed," he told me in a hurry.

Without even saying "hi" or "good morning," he left the room.

Then I had no choice other than to get up and get ready.

Chapter 24

Tahiti, what can I say. This was definitely going to get my mind off of things. We went in our limo to our motel. The driver helped me out. The sun warmed my bare shoulders as I got out.

I looked around. Everyone was looking at us. Alistair got out. He took his sunglasses out of his shirt and put them on. The driver unloaded our bags and brought them into the motel.

We walked around a little bit since there was no need for us to stay at the motel. The driver was setting everything up.

We held hands as we walked down the street. People keep looking at us. I didn't really pay any attention until a boy came up to me. "Hello," he said. He was about my age, maybe a little older.

I looked at him and smiled. "Hi," I replied.

I could tell that Alistair was getting a bit annoyed.

"My name is Jeremy. What's yours?"

I looked at him then over at Alistair. I could tell his eyes getting cold, even under his dark shades. "I'm Natalie. Now if you excuse me. We're kind of busy," I said, meaning Alistair and me.

Jeremy nodded. "Yeah, well, don't be a stranger now. You stick around."

I nodded and waved good-bye as Alistair pulled me away. "If you talk to him again, then I will talk to him as well," Alistair said under his breath.

I had to laugh. "Are you jealous?"

He didn't say anything. I grabbed both of his hands and pulled him down on a bench near us. "You are, aren't you?" I pulled off his glasses. "You look at me in the eye and tell me that you're not jealous."

He looked at me in the eye but didn't say anything. "I'm jealous. Now give me my glasses back. Come, let's go get a drink," he said while grabbing his glasses and pulling me to my feet.

I nodded and followed him to a bar near the beach. We sat down, and a man came over to take our order. "Your orders please," he said.

Alistair looked at me. "Um, just a Coke for now. We'll come back later tonight," he said while smiling at the man.

The bartender looked at Alistair and smiled. "I'll look forward to it." He handed our two glasses and went over to help the other people.

I turned in my seat to face the beach. I watched as people ran and played on the beach. Then I watched as guys surf in the water. I wanted to go down there. In a new bikini, tanning.

Alistair snapped his fingers in front of my face to stop me from zoning out. "You okay there?" he asked me.

I turned to him. "I wanna go to the beach," I told him.

He looked at me and smiled. "Then what are we waiting for? Let's go."

We raced back to the motel. I even think I passed Jeremy on the way there. Since we were good teenagers, we both got our own bedroom. I opened the door and raced over to my luggage. I searched there the pile of bags for my bathing things.

When I found them, I took out my towel, bikini, and sunglasses. I went into the bath and changed in my brown and blue bathing suit. I put my little skirt thing over top and walked out into the hall. There, standing, was Alistair. He didn't look any different. Then I realized that he changed into his trunks.

He looked at me up and down. "Wow."

I looked at him. "How does it look? Bad?"

He shook his head. "No. But let's just say this. Jeremy better not be there."

We walked down the beach and got a private place. I put down my towel laid down. I put my glasses on and started my tanning. "I'm going to see how cold the water is," I heard Alistair tell me as he started to walk away.

I nodded but didn't say anything. I laid there in peace until I felt a bit of sand fly onto my leg. I opened my eyes. I couldn't make out who it was with my glasses on so I took them off. Then I saw Jeremy standing there above me, smiling. "Hi," he said.

I looked at him then sat up. "Oh, hey. How's it going," I asked him.

I guess he thought that was a gesture for him to sit down because he sat down next to me. "Oh, it's going. So what are you doing here?"

"You mean in Tahiti?"

Jeremy nodded obviously. "Oh, um, Alistair and I are just here for a vacation," I told him.

"Yeah, why is your brother always with you?"

"I'm not her brother" came a voice behind him.

I looked up. Alistair was standing there with his towel. "I'm her boyfriend. Pleasure to meet you," he said to Jeremy.

Jeremy stood up. "Oh, please. The pleasure is all mine," he said as he put out his hand to shake Alistair's.

They held each other's hands for a long time. I could see both of their muscles tense as they shake each other's hands.

Finally, they let go, and I just looked at them. "So Alistair, do you know how to surf?" Jeremy asked.

Alistair nodded. "Yep, do you?"

Jeremy nodded while looking off at the water. "You know, the waves are just right. You wanna catch a few waves?"

"Sure."

Before they left, Alistair came down to me and gave me a kiss. "Bye, love."

As they started to walk away I heard Alistair say, "Yeah, I can do that because I'm going *out* with her. Do you have a girlfriend?"

I just stared at them as they hit the water and started paddling with their surfboards.

I put my sun glasses back on and laid back down. I felt the sun warm my body. I think I fell asleep. Because when I woke up, I heard Alistair and Jeremy arguing about something. "No, I'm more experienced," I heard Jeremy say. "I could beat you to a pulp."

Alistair shook his head. I pulled off my glasses. "What's going on?" I asked.

"He thinks he can beat me up," Alistair explained.

I didn't laugh even though I knew that it was impossible for Jeremy to do that. "Really, then why don't you two fight? See who wins," I asked.

I got up and brushed the sand off of my legs. I could feel the guys' eyes on me. "Where are you going?" Alistair asked me.

"I'm going to go get changed then go to get my nails done."

Jeremy smiled. "Okay, hot stuff. We'll see you later."

I just let that one fly. However Alistair didn't. He stood up. "Okay, where and when do you wanna do this thing?" he asked.

Jeremy stood up too. "Well, obviously after Natalie is done with her nails. But after that, on the basketball court. There, everyone will be watching and waiting to see you fail."

Jeremy started to walk past him. He came up to me. "I'll see you later."

As he walked past me, his hand brushed up against my back. I didn't do or say anything until he was gone. "You better beat him or I will," I told Alistair.

I walked away then to my hotel room to get changed. I put on white short and a blue tank top. I put my hair down and returned my glasses to the top of my head.

I walked out of the hotel building down the street to the nail solon. I walked into the place and rang the bell. When no one came out from the back, I sat down. I looked at the magazine. Finally, a lady came out with a smile. "Well, hello. What can I do for you today, miss?" the lady asked.

I told to paint my nail white with a blue strip on it. She had me sit down in the chair as she filed my nail the shined. Then last but not least, she painted them. It didn't take that long, but when I was done, she said, "That will be $65."

I looked at her. "To have my nails done!"

She smiled. "I know who you are. You're like the daughter of Lar Mandel. You have the money so cough it up."

She left me no choice but to pay her ridiculous high price.

I left the place with $65 less. Though I didn't mind. If I wanted more money, I would just ask Alistair. Then I remembered that I was supposed to meet them over at the basketball court to see them fight. This was going to be great.

I never understood guys. They always had to be stronger than each other. I walked fast down the street while admiring my nails. Even though it cost much more than it should have, the lady did a good job.

I finally reached the basketball court. And already a pile of people were standing around, waiting to see what was going to happen.

Alistair was saving me a seat up front.

He gave me a kiss on the cheek as he turned away to go talk to Jeremy. "Okay, you wanted to fight so let's fight. No weapons. Just us," he said. "You ready?"

Jeremy jumped up and down a bit. "Ready as I'll ever be."

Alistair nodded. "Okay, ready, go."

They didn't charge at each other at first. They walked around in a circle. Jeremy was bent down with his fists up. When Alistair was standing up straight, keeping his hands down.

I knew that Jeremy had to have had a reputation by the way the people were yelling. "Come on, Jeremy," they said. "You can do it."

I just sat there quietly, smiling. Finally, Jeremy lunged toward him. Alistair sprinted to the left. Then finally, Jeremy took a swing. Alistair caught Jeremy's hand in his fist then flung him back, making him fall. He turned to look at me. I shrugged and smiled.

Then as Alistair was turned toward me, Jeremy got up and started running toward Alistair. Jeremy put his hand on Alistair's shoulder. Then he took Jeremy's hand and flipped him.

This went on for the next few minutes. Alistair knocking Jeremy down. Making Jeremy get up and then having him fall back down. Finally, Alistair said, "Okay, that's enough. You made your point. You can't fight worth crap. Just let it go before you hurt yourself."

Alistair walked toward me. "Aren't you tired?" I asked him.

He started to push me forward when Jeremy yelled something at me. "Yo, babe. Who is he? Isn't he tired?"

I stopped and turned to look at him. "He wasn't even going medium hard on you. Go to a gym, you'll get better," I told him.

I heard people laugh. "Well, who is he?" Jeremy asked me again.

I looked at him in the eye. "We're part of the Mafia, my friend. It was very nice to meet you."

With that, Alistair and I headed back to our rooms. We didn't know what to do. We went into his room, sat down on the couch, and turned on the TV. I couldn't believe that we were in Tahiti but were in our room watching TV. It didn't seem right. I got up from the couch and walked over to the TV to turn it off. "What are you doing?" Alistair asked me.

I walked over to the door. "Let's go do something," I told him.

He shrugged his shoulders and got off the chair. He grabbed his wallet and followed me out the door.

We came once again, out of the building. "So what do you want to do?" he asked me.

"I don't know. You feel like riding?"

He looked over at the beach and said, "Yeah sure we can ride across the beach."

I nodded. "Okay."

We walked over to the rented stables and talked to the person who worked there. He gave us two horses.

We walked them out onto the grass and looked down at the path to the beach. "Bet I can beat you to the other end of it," Alistair said, meaning, the beach.

I smiled, kicked my legs against the horse, and got a head start. "Hey," he said as he started to run after me.

I smiled as I glided through the air. I looked back. I didn't see him. Then out of nowhere, Alistair ran out in front of me. He laughed, and I went faster. The people of the beach started to cheer us on.

I started to gain on him. Finally, when were right at the neck of each other, I could see where the finishing line was. I pulled to go faster, and I did. I raced out in front of Alistair and crossed the line.

I slowed to a stop. I pulled at the reins and got off. I brushed at my hair with my fingers. Then watched at Alistair was only *now* getting off his horse.

He looked at me as he got off. "Okay, let's do something that I can win at," he said while starting to grin.

"Okay, but what's that?" I started to laugh when he came over and playfully slapped my arm.

"Come on, let's go return these horses."

When we got to the stables, the workman came out. "So she ran for you, did she?" he said, talking about Alistair's horse.

I wanted to laugh but didn't. I took my horse back to its stable. "What do you mean?" Alistair asked curiously.

"I told the miss that she wasn't any good at running. She's getting old, but she insisted on getting you that one."

I could see Alistair looking past the man at me while I was in the stable patting my horse.

"Oh, she did, did she?" Alistair said returning this attention to the man. Anyway, thank you for the horse. How much do I owe you?"

"Um, just make it three even."

Alistair took out his wallet and counted three hundred even. The man saw all of the cash and looked at Alistair. "Who are you?"

Alistair hesitated with his answer. "Um, you know women. Always wanting to shop."

I looked at him and looked at me back. "Yep, I know how you mean. If you have money, they'll take it all."

I came out to meet them, and Alistair said, "Yeah, well nice to meet you." He started to laugh as he took my hand and pulled me away.

When we were far enough away, I started to laugh. "You gave me an old horse," Alistair realized. "Didn't you."

"Well, I didn't want you to win, now did I?" I stated.

I laughed, pulled away, and started to run away. He made a laugh and started to run after me. I knew he was going to catch me, but it didn't matter. Wasn't that the whole point sometimes?

I ran as fast as I could, but then he caught up. He slowed me down and started to tickle me. When he stopped, he said, "Now what?"

I looked at him. "I don't know. You wanna share an ice cream?"

He looked at me. "Okay, but I'm ordering. I don't trust you anymore."

I laughed a little and said, "Okay, I'll go find a seat, and you get it."

He nodded, and he went off. I walked over to the first seat that I found unoccupied. I sat down and just watched as the waves came in and hit the beach.

Soon I felt two hands wrap around my eyes. I didn't think Alistair could have gotten the ice cream that fast but turned away.

In front of me stood Jeremy. He had two other guys with him. "Oh my God. What do you want?" I asked.

He looked down at and sat down. It was funny as to how the other dudes did exactly as he did. He put his hands on the table as did they right after. "So, Miss Mafia. We wanna rematch," he said, sounding so, so stupid.

I looked at him and started to get up. I looked over and saw Alistair walking toward us with the ice cream. "No, you had your chance and you lost it. Besides he would only beat you again."

Alistair came up to us and handed me my (our) ice cream. Jeremy stood up to face me. "Then why don't you fight me? You should know how, don't you? If you beat me, we call it even, but I bet you, you owe me the night."

The other guys behind him laughed. I made a sarcastic chuckle too. Then I wiped off my smile. I looked at my ice cream. I smiled and smashed it into his face. Jeremy closed his eyes. He wiped away his face before he opened them again.

I turned to walk away with Alistair. "There, I beat you, good-bye," I told him.

Then I felt somewhat of a sticky hand grab my shoulder. "It's not over unless I say so."

I took the hand. I bent forward and pulled the hand and the rest of the body with me. Then I seemed to be looking down at Jeremy on the ground.

Alistair got down and started to slam his hand down on the sand next to him. "One, two three," he said. "You're out."

He got up then and took my hand. "There, it's over. And that's a ref's point of view."

We walked away. We headed into town and went back to our rooms. We didn't come out of them for the rest of the day. We just stayed in Alistair's room watching TV. I think we even fell asleep on the couch.

Anyway, we woke up in the morning. It was a perfect time to go down to the beach. I ran into my room. I came back out in my bikini ready to go tan again.

I saw Alistair awake and said, "Come on, let's go."

Alistair got off of the sofa and looked at me. "Okay, but you're not wearing that," he told me.

"What?"

I looked at me and walked over to the door where I was. "I don't need Jeremy coming over and looking at you again. I'm sorry, Natalie, but no."

I looked at him. I didn't say anything but ran into my room. I could hear him following. I closed and locked the door quickly.

I ran onto my bed and started to cry. I couldn't believe was telling me to put a different swimsuit on.

It was like only been the second day here. But for the rest of the time we've been there, we hardly said a word to each other. Jeremy let us alone as we left each other alone.

CHAPTER 25

Since Alistair and I got back from our little vacation—exactly three weeks in Tahiti—I was up in my room. And over the past few days, the house sort of went back to normal. And by "normal," I mean, Mandel making incredible success. He can now walk without crutches. (However when he walks, you can tell that it bothers him. But who could blame him? He was shot. But normally you might still be in the hospital. So he was doing very well for his age.)

Anyway, I was lying on my stomach, reading a book—*A New Life for Everyone*. It was about a girl who was kidnapped to replace a daughter who died.

I rolled onto my back and put the book down beside me. I was reading since nine this morning. It wasn't because I had to but because it was something to do. After the fight between Alistair and me, reading felt like the right thing to do. (Not really.)

I got up and went over to the window. Down on the ground stood Mandel and Alistair. (Behind them, the limo driver was cleaning the car windows.) They were talking. Soon Prinella came out with ice tea. They said something that made Prinella give a little laugh. I made a little chuckle as well.

My eyes then focused over on Alistair. He was laughing. I smiled. Soon he looked my way and saw me in the window looking down at him. He stopped talking for a second. He nodded and smiled at me. He put his hand up for a notion to have me come down and join them. I shook my head and went away from the window.

Alistair put his hand back down and looked over at Mandel. Prinella was on her way back in the house. "Go talk to her, son," Mandel said to him.

Alistair breathed in deeply and nodded. Mandel patted his son on the shoulder as he watched Alistair walk back in the house. He walked up the stairs slowly. Breathing in and letting it out didn't seem to help him being nervous. But why should he have been nervous? He didn't do anything wrong. He looked up; he still had two flights of stairs to climb. He decided to take his time. Besides, Natalie probably wouldn't talk to him anyway . . .

I decided to go down and talk to Alistair. I grabbed my sweatshirt and headed for the door. I didn't know what I was going to say to him, but I knew that I had to make him see how I felt. I didn't even know how we got into this silly fight anyway . . .

Alistair was only half up the first flight of stairs. *Why am I even doing this,* he thought. *I never did anything wrong. She's the one that made me yell at her.* He started to walk faster.

I came to the stairway. I started to go down slowly but sped up as I realized that I had nothing to lose. He was the one that made me yell and walk away. I never did anything. If he didn't tell me to shut up and go away, this never would have happened.

He finally made it to the second flight of stairs. He looked up. There, in the middle of the stairway, stood Natalie. He looked at her with concerned eyes. She looked back at him with an out-of-your-mind expression.

There he stood. Before me with hesitant eyes. All I wanted to do was go back to my room and lock the door. However, I kept walking. I looked down past Alistair. There at the bottom of the stairs, I saw Mandel looking up at us. He smiled and nodded.

I can't believe she's looking at me like that, thought Alistair. Such hatred in her eyes against me. And I didn't even do anything! Alistair continued to walk up the stairs but slowed down for he didn't want to be the one who met Natalie first.

Only a few steps away from Alistair, and I knew what I was going to do. I walked faster. Only a matter of time until I would have passed Alistair. He was now looking at me with understanding eyes. Only when I passed him, that face turned to the complete opposite.

I made it the bottom of the steps before him. I raced across the floor, past Mandel and outside. I skipped over the limo. "Take me on a drive please," I asked the driver.

The man nodded politely but down the bucket and went over to the stairs to get his hat. Meanwhile, Alistair came out of the house and raced over to where I was.

By the time I saw him and tried to get into the vehicle, he had my arm. I tried to pull away, but it was no use. The driver started to rush toward us. Alistair pulled me away from the limo and held his arm up to the man. Soon the limo driver nodded and went back to his cleaning.

Alistair pulled me across the perfectly laid stone on the driveway. I looked over at the house. Standing outside of it was Mandel. Who indeed was now spying on us. I tried to run free. But no matter how hard I tried to kick or hit, it was obvious that Alistair got more out of boot camp than I did.

He dragged me over to the far side of the pond. There he pushed me down on an old tree stump. I looked up at him with defeat. I look in a deep breath and let it out. "What?" I yelled.

I started to get up. Hoping that he would just let me walk away. But instead he pushed me back down. "Okay, I'm the guy, and guys are supposed to be the stronger one so shut up and listen to what I have to say," he said.

There he goes again about the shut up, I thought. "Don't even think about telling me to shut up again. You remember where it got you the last time."

He didn't say anything. "We need to talk about what happened last night."

I scoffed. "Now you're acting as if we're married. We're only sixteen and seventeen."

He sighed. "That maybe, but I have a feeling that we're going to be stuck with each other for a little while longer. And I know that right now we both hate each other's guts, but we need to at least discuss what happened last night."

I stood up, only then did I realize how tall he was. He wasn't aggressively taller than me, but you could tell that compared to him, I was short. I would say that he was around five feet, six inches. When I, on the other hand, was only five feet two inches.

I don't know why I'm even telling you this. It has nothing to do with what's going on. I looked at him in the eye. "It wasn't only last night. It was like the whole time we were in Tahiti. You acted like you own me. I'm not to be bought. I thought you knew that. But I guess you don't because you hardly ever talk to me."

He looked at me with understanding. "I see. Well, I saw how you were looking over at that guy, Jeremy. I'm a guy, Natalie, I'm going to get jealous."

I had to think this through. "So let me get this straight, you were jealous. And I wasn't looking over at him. He was looking at me. And you know that."

He nodded shyly. I could tell he was a little embarrassed to tell me that. "I thought guys don't get jealous."

"Yeah."

"Okay, fine but that doesn't explain why you were telling me what to wear. You didn't even let me wear the bathing suit that I wanted. You were acting like we were married and that you owned me. That's not cool."

He took in a deep breath. "I guess I was, wasn't I?"

I nodded. "Well *just* a little."

I started to walk away when he grabbed my hand. He pulled me back, "I love you." He smiled at me. "I do," he reassured me.

I sighed. "Yep."

I pulled away and started to walk away again. "Well," he called after me.

"Love you too," I yelled behind me.

I looked back, and he was sitting on the tree stump, smiling at me. I smiled as well. I walked past the pond and through the garden. When I reached the house, I saw Mandel sitting on the porch steps.

I started to jog over to him. He stood up and greet me. He had a smile on his face. I slowed down and walked up and gave him a hug. "Thanks," I said.

I pulled apart and continued to walk inside the house. "What for?" he asked.

I stopped and turned around. "For everything you did."

I walked into the cool house. Prinella was walking my way with a tray of ice tea. She stopped in front of me and handed me a glass. "Miss," she said as she smiled and curtsied.

I smiled as I said, "Thank you."

Even though I wasn't exactly in the happiest mood, no one was to know. I know that Alistair said that he *loved* me. I knew that he didn't. Well, I thought he didn't. If he did, he could have showed it a lot better. The definition of *love* is a tender affection for somebody *or* to feel romantic and sexual desire and longing for somebody. I know that you might not agree, but hey, that's what the dictionary says.

I strolled back up to my room to read more of my book, *A New Life for Everyone*. I opened the door and hopped on my bed. I picked up the book and read: *Everyone has their own reason for liking or disliking people. Some reasons are better than others. Around where I lived, my neighbors had a big grudge about towel heads (Arabs). I don't know if it's because they're terrorists or just because they were different. I was raised to hate them. But as I got older, I came to love them. But that's only because I grew up with them after the age of fifteen.*

I am now nineteen and I still live with them in Morocco. And for the last four years, I have not known them for nothing but plain ordinary people. Normally, I wouldn't be allowed to write a story like this about them, but I promised my father that I would do nothing but tell the truth.

I miss my American family immensely, but I have a new one now. The way I became Vashti Muhand I will never forget. And I write it down for other people to understand how I feel.

I have learned so much since I lived with my father (Jahar Muhand). I learned to speak six languages fluently (Arabic, Hebrew, French, Latvian, Swedish, and German). I learned a lot of European cultures, and I have traveled all around the world.

When in America with my mom, she always wished that I would have brothers, sisters, and a father who would care about me. And even though it wasn't how she wanted it, I got it.

From what I said so, far you might take this as me saying that I don't like my American family. But I do. I love them more now than I ever did. But no matter how much l love and miss them, it wouldn't do me any good. Unless my father lets me see her, I don't.

I was interrupted by a knock on the door. Instead of just saying for them to come in, I actually walked over and opened it up. I turned the knob and saw Yassen standing there, looking at me.

I just stared at him. He wasn't supposed to be here. He was supposed to be on a mission in the Netherlands. "Yassen," I said with a surprised tone. "What are you doing here?"

Yassen walked in a closed door without saying anything. "Hush, Mandel doesn't know that I'm back. I want it to be a surprise," he said.

I looked into his eyes. Something was wrong. He didn't look normal, there was something in his eyes. "Oh, well, it's good to have you back," I said with a lack of enthusiasm.

He looked at me. "Is something wrong, Natalie? Everything okay with you and Alistair?"

I took in a deep breath, "Yeah, everything is great. Well I need to go and do something."

I stretched out to give him a hug and started to walk out of the room. "It's great to have ya back," I said before I left the room.

Yassen watched as Natalie went out. Yep, it's great to have me back. Just wait for the surprise. I'm sure that you'll think that it's good to have me back.

I walked down stairs and saw Alistair just walking in. I didn't wanna tell Mandel about Yassen being back because it would ruin the surprise. But I guess it would be okay to tell him. I walked toward Alistair. "Can we talk?" I asked.

Thinking that I meant about talking about us, Alistair took my hand and pulled me into the study. He then sat down in the chair and pulled me on top of his knee.

I sighed. "Okay, so what's up?" he asked.

"It's about Yassen."

Alistair looked at me, puzzled. "But he's shouldn't be back yet, he's supposed to be on a mission."

I nodded. "I know, but he was up in my room. I don't know where he is now."

Alistair looked away. "Well, let's go and tell Father."

He started to push me up when I pushed him back down. "No, Yassen said that it was a surprise."

He nodded, "Well, let's go talk to him."

I shrugged. "Okay, he's up in my room."

I then got off this lap and followed him up stairs. He would look over at me every couple of steps. I didn't know what he was thinking, and even though I wanted to know, I was kind of scared. From what I knew about guys before this, they can be very *visual.* I don't know if that's good or bad. I guess it all depends.

We came to the hallway of my room. The door was closed. Alistair went to open it. In the room sat Yassen holding something. I couldn't see it at first. I wanted to go into the room, but Alistair held me back at the door way. "Yassen," he said in an orderly tone.

I didn't know what there was to be afraid of. So what if he finished with his mission early. That doesn't mean that we need to take security action, but I just stood there as Alistair had me.

Yassen looked over and held up the object. In his hands were a little puppy. A Shih Tzu. As if a miracle, my face lit up. I pulled away from Alistair and raced toward the dog. "He's for you. I got him in the Netherlands," Yassen said.

Alistair walked in calmly. "So you were spending time in the Netherlands to get a dog for Natalie. Very considerate. But did you finish what you were supposed to?" Alistair asked coldly.

Yassen handed me the dog and stood up to face Alistair. "Yes, sir. I did finish the mission, and I had a couple of days so I thought that I would pick up a little present for Natalie. Why should that concern you?"

Alistair looked at him. "If you did what you had to do, then I have nothing to say."

Yassen smiled. "Well, it has been done."

Alistair smiled back at him. "Then, my friend there is nothing left to say other than welcome home. For now anyway."

They walked toward each other and shook hands. I smiled then went back to playing with the dog. "So what are you going to name it?" asked Alistair.

I looked at him then at the dog. It was so cute. It was white and had brown blotches on the cheeks. "I don't know. What do you think?"

They both looked at the dog with high concentration. "It's your dog."

"I don't know. I'll have to think about it."

I continued to smile and play with the dog. I heard Yassen give a little chuckle as he turned to leave. "Where are you going?" I asked.

"To rest and freshen up before dinner. See you two then."

We both said bye, and Alistair came over to sit next to me on the bed.

Until dinner, we both continued to play with the dog that was by then named Shadow. I don't know why I picked that name but I found out that being in the dark shadow makes really big shadows. But anyway, the dog's name is now Shadow.

CHAPTER 26

Six o'clock came before we knew it, and we weren't dressed. A knock came at the door, and in came Prinella. "Miss, Mr. Mandel would like me to remind you to be down for dinner," the maid said.

I put the dog down and stood up. "Thank you; tell him I'll be down directly," I said.

Prinella smiled then looked over at Alistair. "He say that it goes for you too."

Alistair nodded while smiling. Prinella smiled, curtsied, and then left the room. Alistair got up and looked up at me. "Well, I better go and get dressed quickly."

I nodded. "Yep, I'll see ya in a few."

I waited to Alistair to leave before I went to pick out a dress. Mandel was always really picky on what we wore to dinner. But I didn't think he would mind if I wore a casual blue summer dress. I put my hair up in a ponytail and painted my nails. Normally I would have gotten a shower, had my hair done, and everything. But today, I didn't feel like it. So Mandel was just going to have to deal with it. (You can't expect a girl to be pretty all the time.)

I walked out into the hallway thinking about what Mandel's expression when he finds out that Yassen was home already. I took my time walking down the steps. Soon I heard pounding behind me. I stopped and turned and found Alistair running toward me. "What happened?" I asked him.

He came to a slow walk and said, "Why do you think something happened?"

He linked my arm in his. "Well, you were running."

"It didn't mean that there was something wrong. I just wanted to catch up with you and walk you to dinner."

So formal, I thought. "Oh, okay. How nice of you to think of that."

He nodded in an honored kind of way.

We came to the double doors that hid the dining room from us. Alistair pushed the door open and rejoined my arm in his. There at the far end of the table sat Mandel. He smiled at us and stood up. "Well, Natalie, why, don't you look pretty," he complimented.

I smiled and said thank you. Then Mandel turned to Alistair who was wearing a dark blue designer sports jacket with light blue jeans. "And Alistair, don't you look so . . . unique."

Alistair looked at his father and smiled. "Thanks," he said.

Mandel motioned with his hands to have us sit down next to him. We did as he asked.

He put up his hands to show us that we may eat. "Wait," I said.

Mandel looked at me. I could tell that he was sort of stunned when I interrupted him. "We have another guest," I told him.

Alistair and I looked at the door. The doors opened and in walked Yassen. I looked over at Mandel's face. His expression was a mixture of shock and misunderstanding. Yassen walked in looking straight at Mandel. He stopped in front of the table.

Mandel just looked at him, as if analyzing him. Then I just knew he approved because he nodded and smiled. Yassen smiled back and walked up to our side of the table. I got up and moved my place over next to Alistair so that Yassen could sit next to Mandel. Like he did before he left.

Then once again, Mandel put up his hands, and we began to eat. We talked a bit at the table. But none of the conversations neared to why Yassen was home so early.

I was the first one to be excused. Instead of staying down having wine and talking about worldwide politics, I decided to head for my room and play with Shadow.

Up in my room was lonely. I was back in my pajamas. I wasn't about to stay in that dress. Dresses are nice but not when all you want to do is chill out.

I played with Shadow until eight in the evening. Soon Alistair joined me. He had a smile on his face as he walked in and closed the door. "So how did the discussion on the problems in Afghanistan go?" I asked.

He scratched his head. "Well, I learned that the Afghans speak up to seventy languages," he informed me. "I think that's what they said. I don't have a clue."

"Oh, how very interesting."

He raised his eyebrow then gave a little chuckle.

We both played with Shadow for the next couple of minutes. Then the door opened slightly. "Yes," I said.

The door opened the rest of the way. "Um, Miss, Mr. Mandel would like you to help me clean up Carlos's room," Prinella said.

I looked at her in silence. Then my eyes switched over to Alistair. He nodded. "I'll be there directly," I answered.

She nodded and closed the door behind her. I looked down at Shadow. His eyes were full of innocence. I got up and put the dog on the bed next to Alistair. "Hey, take it easy," he said.

I looked back at him. "I know," I said, acting fine.

I wasn't fine. I know that it sounds silly, but I still wasn't over with what happened. I don't think that anyone could ever get over it. Especially if he or she was a good friend. I walked slowly to the door. I walked out into the hallway. Taking a left down the hall, I thought about the good times with Carlos. We always seemed to get along.

Soon, I came to Carlos's room. I hesitantly opened the door. Inside I saw two maids cleaning the curtains and dusting. Prinella came toward me with two boxes of stuff. "This is for you to look through," she said as she handed me two heavy boxes.

I took to boxes and went over to the bed. I sat down and took something out of the first box. It was a baseball glove. I remembered the first time that he ever used it. It was the summer that he turned eleven. I got it for him. He didn't know how to use it, well, not very well. But he learned. He became very good actually.

Putting the glove down, I picked up something else. This time it was a picture. Of him and me. We were posing after we got all dirty on a camping trip. We were young, like, nine. But we had fun. It was funny to what I would do to go back to those days.

I went through about everything that was in the first box. The second box was filled with nothing but stuff animals and pictures. I took everything out. However at the bottom was a letter. Then I remember what it was. It was the paper that Carlos gave to me. I opened it and read it carefully:

Natalie and Alistair,
   Didn't want to tell you this orally for fear that someone might be listening in. So I tell you this now. Yassen is not to be trusted. He might seem nice. But really he was on Mandel #2's side. And

he is now the one that you should be afraid of. Don't let him hurt
Dad or Natalie. Alistair, I need you to watch him carefully. Try
to find out what he's going to do. Tell Father when you think the
time is right. But remember, no matter how nice Yassen is, don't
trust him. Don't ask me how I found this out. I just knew.

~ Carlos

I read the letter over and over again. I couldn't believe what I
read. After all of these years of Yassen supposedly helping Mandel,
he was really only doing that to get his trust so he could destroy
him. I had to show Alistair this. I got off the bed, raced past all the
maids, and ran out the door. How did Carlos know this? And why
didn't I read it earlier?

As I was walking swiftly to my room, I spotted Yassen down the
hall. He saw me and waved. Hiding the letter, I waved and put a
smile on my face. "Hey, Natalie, where are you going?" he asked
me with a smile.

"Oh, to my room," I said with hesitation.

"Is something wrong? Do you wanna talk about something?"

I looked at him. He looked at me. There was silence.

He knew that I found out. He sighed then gave me a scary smile.
Then he turned around and started to walk fast down the hall.

I watched him disappear down the hall and around the bend.
Then I started back to my room again. I opened the door and
slammed it shut.

Alistair saw the seriousness in my face. "Is everything okay?" he
said.

"Yassen never really was on that mission," I told him.

Alistair looked at me with disbelief. "How do know that?"

Without saying anything, I handed the letter to him. He read
it twice like I did. He looked at me, furious. "We got to tell my
father."

He started to race toward the door. I knew nothing but to follow
him. We ran down the stairs. We paced the maids to the study. The
door was closed, and I saw Mandel in there, reading. He always
read after dinner. In fact, he never liked to be disturbed. But under
certain circumstances, I don't think he would mind.

Alistair pushed open the door. Mandel looked up and took off
his glasses. "Son, what is it?" he asked in a casual voice.

Mandel leaded back in his chair and crossed his arms. Alistair said nothing but gave him the letter. Mandel started to open it but looked at us first. We nodded. He sighed and read it. He didn't say anything for five minutes. All he did was stare at the piece of paper.

I wanted to know what was going on in his head. Frankly, I might be a little scared. Well, to know what might be going on in someone like Mandel's head. If that makes any sense. Anyhow, I'm having second thoughts on wanting to know what Mandel might be thinking about.

Mandel took a deep breath. "Well," I said, waiting for a response. I couldn't believe that he was so quiet. "Why is he so quiet?" I asked Alistair quietly.

"He's thinking," he answered, talking into my ear.

"Oh," I said while nodding.

Mandel sat up in his chair. "Where is he?"

I sighed. "Um, when I was walking to my room to show Alistair, I saw him in the hall. He came up to me and asked me if anything was wrong. Then he stared at me, as if he knew that I found out. Then he ran down the hall."

"Okay, and when was this?" Mandel asked.

I calculated in my head about how many minutes ago this happened. "About twenty minutes ago. God, he could be halfway across Latvia," I said.

"But he wouldn't, would he? He seems to be like M2. He doesn't run," Alistair said.

I just stood there listening and learning contently. "Yes, son, I think you're right. Get a hold of the team," Mandel told Alistair.

"Wait. What? You have a team? You never told me this," I clarified.

Alistair looked at me. "Well, we do."

Mandel stood up. "Natalie, I'll explain everything to you later, but right now we have work to do," he said.

Alistair started toward the phone. "What can I do?" I asked.

Mandel stopped in front of me and put his hands on my shoulders. "My dear, you may get ready for battle."

Now when he said battle, I don't really think he meant *battle*. But I didn't know that at the time.

I looked at him. "Battle?"

He smiled. "Yes, now upstairs in *my* room, there is a case on the table. Inside is something I think you should have if you're going to be part of this family."

I looked at him, trying to figure out what game he's trying to play. I did as he said and headed up to his room. I felt kind of honored to being allowed to go in his room. I never was before. I guess with everything going on, there were some exceptions allowed to be made.

I made it to the top of the steps and walked down the west hall to his room. The door was big. I opened it and I walked into a huge room. I mean, huge. The first part of the room was bigger than my whole room put together. And what I saw, there were two more parts.

I found the table the he was talking about. And there on it was as he described, the case. I recognized it. I walked over to it. Yes, it was very familiar. I opened it up. There in front of me was a gun. The same gun that the guy gave to me when he first told me that my parents were dead.

I picked up the gun—Glock. I held it in my hands for a long time. Then I took it downstairs to show Mandel.

I walked into the library to find Alistair on the phone, yelling. There on the other end on the room sat Mandel looking at a piece of paper. "Ah, you found it. Good."

I looked at him then at the weapon. "What's this for?" I asked.

He smiled. "So you can defend yourself."

Again I looked at him. "Why would I need to defend myself?"

"So Yassen doesn't hurt you when we go to catch him."

I thought back to when he asked me to join the Mafia. "But you said that I wouldn't have to kill anyone."

He nodded in agreement. "Yes, I did say that. But that was almost a year ago, maybe more. You're older. Besides I don't think you have a choice. This is about all of us. And you don't have to kill. What do you think we are, murderers?"

I thought about it for a few minute and knew that he was right. "But I don't know how to shoot one of these things," I said, meaning, the gun.

"That's okay, tomorrow Alistair can give you a short lesson, can't you, Alistair?" Mandel said, looking over at his son.

Over at the phone sat Alistair. "No! You don't understand, I need to talk him. No, ma'am. Just give him the phone and tell him it's Alistair. Yes, yes, my name is Alistair!"

Mandel and I just looked at him. Alistair turned toward us. "Now, since my name is Alistair, she'll let me talk to him."

"You will show Natalie how to shoot a gun tomorrow, right?" Mandel asked him.

Alistair looked at me and smiled. "Yeah, sure, no problem. Oh, Mr. Hodgins, yes, it's Alistair," he said, continuing on with his conversation over the phone.

"Well, there you have it, you'll learn to shoot a gun tomorrow. Now you can go up to bed and get some sleep because in two days, we will be looking for my former friend."

I nodded. I stretched out to give Mandel a hug. Then as I was leaving the room, I walked over to Alistair and gave his a little kiss on the cheek. He looked at me as I walked away, and I smiled.

I walked up to my room like I did many times today. I couldn't believe that in a few days, I will sort of hunt my first person with the Mafia. In fact, with the Mafian team. Now who can say that?

I walked in my room and over to my bed. I laid on my bed and flipped on the TV. I put on Animal Planet. I don't know how many channels there were, but I could tell you that they had channels in a least two languages. Now to me that's impressive.

I believe I feel asleep with the TV on because when I woke up, it was talking about how many different types of snake there are in South America. I looked over at my alarm clock. It read eight o'clock.

I hopped out of bed and went into the bathroom to get a shower and brush my teeth. I came out of the bathroom in my bathrobe. A pounding came from the door. In walked Alistair dressed in blue jeans and a black shirt. That made him look totally hot, by the way. He had his hair a certain way that made me wanna . . . well, never mind.

I looked at him. Not even noticing what he had in his hand. He held up a cup of coffee. I guess I was too busy looking at his cloths. I don't know what was going on with me. It normally didn't matter what he had on. I guess I should pay more attention to what he's wearing. Or maybe not.

"Good," he said as he walked over to me. He put the cup in my hand and gave me a kiss on the cheek and finished. "Morning."

Holding the cup of coffee in my bathrobe, I stared at him. Maybe something was wrong with him too. Me only now realizing how good he dresses, and him only now treating me like I was his girlfriend. Seems like a good day to me.

He backed away and looked at me. "I think you better get something else on if you wanna shoot."

I looked at him. What was he talking about? Why do I need to get dressed? It's only eight in the morning. However within the time I took my shower and Alistair came in, it was going on nine.

"What are you talking about?" I asked.

Alistair raised an eyebrow. "Don't tell me you forgot. Yassen, the gun. Training? Anything."

I took a sip of coffee then remembered. Alistair was going to teach me how to shoot. "Ooh. Yeah, so when are we going to start?"

Alistair looked at me then eyed my bathrobe. "Well, as soon as you can get dressed into something more, um, civilized."

I looked down at my morning wear. I didn't know why this would have been termed as *uncivilized*, but I did understand that I should get dressed before I shoot a gun.

CHAPTER 27

I was really excited. For the first time in my life, I was going to shoot a gun. But I have to admit. I was kind of scared. I came out of my room in jeans and a sweatshirt.

I walked downstairs. I could smell bacon and eggs. Umm. I walked into the kitchen. There standing at the table was Alistair. He looked at me and started to walk toward me. He walked past me while grabbing my arm. "Hey, what are you doing?" I asked him.

"If you wanna shoot a gun, then you need practice. You don't have time to eat," he said.

I sighed and let him pull me away. As we passed by Prinella bringing Mandel's breakfast, I saw a piece of toast. I grabbed it as we walked out of the room. Alistair saw what I did and laughed. "What?" I asked while eating the toast.

"You're pitiful. But cute," he explained.

He let go of my arm, and we both walked outside. We walked behind the house and past the basketball court. Then I saw seven targets. Not like the ones you would it you were doing archery, but they were showing a person from the waist on up. And they were in different.

Alistair took his gun out from in his shirt. He aimed for the head of the target thing and shot. I quickly covered my ears. Even though I heard a gun go off before, it was louder than I expected up close.

He put the gun down and looked at me. "You think you can do that?" he asked me.

I looked at him then the target. How could I miss? All you do is point the gun in the direction. "Oh, of course I can. How hard can it be?" I answered him.

He raised his eyebrows and handed me *my* gun. "Now, remember to aim. And don't forget that it gives off a little kick."

I nodded. I pulled the gun up in front of me. I aimed and pulled the trigger. The gun made a pop, and then I saw a hole in the target. I looked at it. Alistair pushed a button that made the target slide up to us. As it came closer, I saw where it hit. Right on the edge of the arm was a small hole. I then looked over at where Alistair hit. Exactly in the middle of the head. I looked at my gun. "I think I'll need to practice a little more," I said.

He smiled reassuringly. "Don't worry. You have all day. And however long Father gives you."

I nodded. "Thank God."

He patted my shoulder and started to walk away. I turned around and yelled. "Where are you going?"

I stopped and turned to face me. "Inside. Don't worry, I'll be back in a little bit."

I sighed and nodded. I pulled the gun up again as I aimed for the target again. It was harder than it looked. Even if you did point at the thing you wanna shoot, it doesn't go there.

I stood there for three minutes just aiming. Making sure that I was going to hit the heart. Or you know, the chest of the person thing. I pulled my finger back and jumped. I grabbed the gun in my other hand. Alistair was right; the thing did kick back. I shook my hand for a little then continued to practice.

Yassen stood there quietly. Waiting in the brush to get a good shot. He couldn't let Natalie live now, he thought. She knew too much. She would rat on him and tell Mandel about who he really was. He wasn't about to let that happen. He pulled up his shotgun. He put it up against his shoulder. He watched and aimed as Natalie practiced her shooting. He grew to love that girl like his own daughter. But she knew too much. It wasn't his fault. She was the one who saw the letter. She was the one who decided to make this happen.

Natalie turned around to "reload" he gun. Yassen stood quietly, aiming, breathing as quietly as he could. He didn't want to do this, but he knew that it was something that had to be done.

Sweat was dripping down his face. He was ready.

I reloaded my gun. Or my *Glock* if you wanna be technical about it. I don't even know if "reload" is the correct term, but I put more bullets in.

I turned to face the cardboard person. I aimed and pulled the trigger. At the same time, I heard a rustle in the bushed up on the hill behind me.

Yassen aimed and shot. He watched at the stray bullet went right past her. She moved. Then he quickly turned and ran off into the trees.

I quickly turned and knelt down on the ground aiming my gun in the direction of the noise. When I saw no one, I got up. I didn't move. I kept quiet still trying to see if I could hear anything. Then I saw Alistair running toward me. "They spotted Yassen running down the hill. Are you okay?" he asked me with his hand on my shoulder.

Thinking about what he just said, I realized what could have happened. "Yeah, I'm fine," I answered in shock.

"What happened?"

I shrugged my shoulders. "I don't know. I heard a noise in the bushes but didn't think to see what was going on. I was practicing, I shot. But after I shot, another gun went off, and I quickly ducked down. Then you came out."

He nodded. "Okay, we need at look out around the perimeter of the house," Alistair said into an earpiece.

He looked at me. "Okay, you come with me," he said while reaching out his arm.

At the time, I didn't know what danger I was in. I didn't think that I could have died right there and then.

Alistair walked inside. "Okay, you go up to your room and stay there."

I nodded and ran up the steps to my room. I walked in the room and sat on the bed. I laid the gun down in the case. I stared at it.

Alistair walked down the one hallway past the kitchen. Took a left and walked over to a wall. He pressed on a painting. Then a little rectangle appeared. He then typed in a code, and the rectangle opened a metal door. Alistair walked through it. He was in a small hallway. He made a left. In front of him was a big metal door. He put the same code into a pad as he did before. The monitor beeped, and the door opened.

Inside the room was Mandel and three other gentlemen. Mandel looked at his son. "What news?" he asked directly.

"Yassen is here," Alistair responded.

Mandel stood up. "In the house," he questioned apprehensively.

"No, but he is in the area. He just made a target at Natalie. She's in her room now."

Mandel nodded. "Ok—"

He was interrupted by gunshots. "Get down!" A man said from upstairs.

Mandel looked up then at his son. "He's in the house and he has help."

"I'll get Natalie!"

Mandel followed his son. "This is Mandel, we have the target on sight. Get back up now," Mandel radioed in his wristwatch.

Alistair ran up the hallway. He typed in the code and reentered the house by walking in through the wall with the painting. He loaded his gun and had it pointing straight ahead. He heard noises. He walked slowly and quietly over to the door of the room. He looked out the window that was next to it. There in the front hall stood Yassen with five other guys. He motioned in front of him to go to the left. He had more than five guys. Alistair watched at the man Yassen sent came his way. He backed away from the window and into a closet. He closed the door behind him.

The man walked in slowly and had his gun out in front of him. Alistair waited to make his move. The man walked toward Alistair. Alistair breathed in deeply and let out. He looked down at the ground. The shadow of where the man's feet were right in front of him.

Alistair took one last breath. Surely, his father was out in the hall by now. Alistair pointed the gun in the middle of the door and pulled the trigger. The sound let out a loud bang. He heard something hit the ground on the other side of the door. He opened it and saw the man on the ground.

I kept hearing shots and noises. I took my gun from the case and walked over into the closet. I was scared and didn't know what was going on. Yassen had to be in the house.

Alistair quickly ran out of the room and toward the stairs. He was running. Soon another shot came. However, the person who dropped was him. Alistair reached for his shoulder. He tripped spun around and fell down the stairs. At the bottom stood Yassen. Still holding up the gun that shot Alistair.

Alistair tumbled to the bottom of the stairs. Soon Yassen heard Mandel's voice coming from another room. He himself raced up the stairs to *Natalie's* room. Mandel ran toward his son on the floor. Then he spotted Yassen at the top. He took three shots and missed all of them. "After him," Mandel told two of his men. The two men went upstairs after him.

Mandel bent down to Alistair. "I'm fine," he told his dad.

"Okay, I'm going to talk to someone. The house is secure, and I sent two guys up after Yassen."

Mandel got up and walked over to the front door.

Yassen walked down the hall. He heard the men after him. He had to get rid of them. Yassen took a left into a random room. Carlos's actually. He took a second to take a glance at it. He remembered the times when he would come in here to talk and have a good time.

But this wasn't one of those times. And those times were over. He paid attention to the door. He put his ear up against it. He listened carefully waiting for when Mandel's *help* was going to pass this room. He heard them down the hall. They passed the room and walked down the hallway.

Yassen quietly opened the door. And walked after them soundlessly. Once he knew that he would make it, he ran up and talked the one guy. The other one was too confused to do anything. Soon Yassen had the one guy out. Then took his gun and wacked the guy up across the head.

He dragged them to the side of the hall and continued onto his original destination—Natalie's room.

I didn't hear anything. I thought they got him. I quietly and slowly turned the closet door handle. I walked out of the closet and over to the window. I saw Mandel walking down the front porch steps. Where was he going? I stayed there, looking out.

Yassen came to Natalie's door. He slowly turned the knob. He pushed the door open and stood there.

I backed away from the window and turned around. I gasped and jumped back. I looked into Yassen's eye. They were cold and deadly. "So how was your day?" he asked me.

I stared at him. I couldn't speak. Then he dared toward me. I screamed. I grabbed my gun and ran the other way.

Alistair winced. He heard Natalie's scream. He applied pressure to his shoulder but putting his hand on it. He got up and walked as fast as he could up the stairs. Again Natalie screamed. Alistair looked up at the top of the stairs. He started to run. He tripped a little from getting off balance but made it.

He held my arms. I struggled to get loose. Finally, using my brain, I kicked him in the crotch. He let go of my arms, and I started to run again. I darted out of the room and down the hall. I made it to the top of the stairs. "Alistair," I yelled.

Alistair looked up at me. Then I felt a hand go around my mouth. I tried to scream, but it came out muffled.

Yassen walked me downstairs, staring at Alistair. Alistair was bent over, trying to catch his breath. Yassen pulled me to the opposite side of Alistair. He walked up to Alistair and did and upper cut to his face. Alistair fell back onto the steps.

I tried to get loose to go and help him, but Yassen dragged me on. "Catch me if you can," he spat at Alistair.

CHAPTER 28

Yassen dragged me out and into a limo nearby. "Take us where I want," he told a man at gunpoint.

The man nodded and got in. Then Yassen shoved me in too. I slid in the seat. Yassen jumped in and closed the door. "Now, go out to the driveway and make a left," he said again with the gun to the driver's head.

We came out to the drive way and make a left like Yassen said. We were going way over the speed limit, but I didn't think Yassen was about to have the man slow down.

"What are you going to do?" I finally asked.

It took a while for Yassen to answer. "I'm not going to do anything. Whatever happens to you from here on out, it will be because of you."

I swallowed. Trying to keep a conversation. "What are you talking about?"

"Don't worry about it. Just do what I say, and you'll live for the next couple of hours. If not, your life will come to an abrupt end."

I didn't bother to ask any other questions because I listened to what he just said. "When should I make a turn?" the driver said in an upfront manner.

"You turn when I tell you to!" Yassen yelled.

The driver nodded perversely and looked straight ahead.

I watched Yassen carefully trying to see if there was any way possible for him to be playing a joke. But for this to be a joke, it would take a miracle so I looked straight ahead.

Alistair lifted his head. He shook it and looked around. Then he jumped up while wincing. His arm hurt badly. (Of course it did. He got shot) He walked over to the front door. Both limos were gone. He looked back inside. The house was a wreck. He walked from room to room to see if there was anyone there. Everyone he saw was either dead or wounded.

The echo of his footsteps floated throughout the house. Then he remembered. Natalie. As fast as he could, he ran to the phone. "Dad. Dad," he yelled into the phone.

"Yeah," a person said on the other line.

"Natalie's missing. I was out of it I couldn't do anything."

There was a silence on the phone. "Okay, we'll be home directly."

With his father's final comment, Alistair hung up. He walked out of the parlor. He went into the bathroom and got out disinfectant out of the medicine cabinet. He unbuttoned his shirt and put the disinfectant onto a cotton pad. He closed his eyes as he quickly laid the pad onto his arm and pressed hard.

Alistair took off the pad and looked in the mirror. It was still bleeding. He took a small towel and tied it around the wound. He winced as he made it tighter. He waited for about five minutes then took it off. He looked down at it. He went over to the shower. He took the shower's head off and turned on cold water. He poured water over it. Then he put a bandage around it and put his shirt back on.

He looked at himself in the mirror then walked out of the room. He went into the study and sat down in the chair behind the desk. He opened a drawer and pulled out a little box. Inside were packs of cartridges. He took out his gun that was still in his shirt. He loaded it and put the box back and stood up.

He heard a vehicle come into the driveway and pull up beside the house. Alistair looked at the door. His father stood there. "Time to go."

Now, to you this may see very dramatic. But in this business, nothing can get too dramatic. I mean, like, it's sort of like a war. There's one side and then the other. They must always be on their guard. And then the time comes when they fight. Our side was getting ready to fight.

I stayed quiet as we still raced down the road to Yassen's wanted destination. We were driving for about two hours now. Occasionally, I would look over at him. Who was he? Before, I always saw a sweet, caring, agreeable, thoughtful, and fun friend. But now I saw, hatred, revenge, and emptiness in him. How could he turn into this? He scared me. I never thought that it would come to this. After all we've been through together. He saved my life many times. And now, he's the one trying to end it.

"Go faster," Yassen yelled at the driver.

The driver quivered. "We're going twenty over the speed. I can't go faster" was the man's answer.

I closed my eyes. "You think I care about how fast we're going? Go faster!"

The driver nodded as I sat up. "Stop this nonsense. Why are you doing this?" I asked Yassen while yelling.

Yassen sat back and turned his head to look at me. I looked into his eyes. They were dead. I sat back and looked out of the window. The windows were black; it was hard for me to see anything.

Yassen smiled. "Did you say anything, Natalie? I'm sorry, I didn't hear you." I shook my head. "No, you must have said something. Did you hear her say something, driver?"

I looked over at the driver. While looking in the review mirror, the driver took in a deep breath. "No, no, I did not." He said, and his voice cracked.

"Are you sure? Because I thought I heard something—"

"Okay, I asked why you're doing this," I budded in.

He smiled. "I will answer your question, Natalie, but not here."

He sat back then, and everything was quiet for the rest of the ride there.

Mandel stood there in the doorway. "Are you ready for this?" he asked his son.

Alistair looked at his father. This is what he's been trained for his whole life. To bust M2. But now that he's gone, his business is with Yassen. So yes, he was ready. He nodded.

"Okay, then let's do this. I called in Monsieur Vague. He will meet us at M2's house in about six hours."

Alistair nodded and they both headed out to the car.

The turned around and headed left down the road. It would take about three hours to catch up to Yassen.

Two more hours went by when we started to go up a hill. When we came to the top my mouth dropped open. In front of us was about a five-story mansion. It was like a castle. Around the house I saw men walking back and forth. They held automatic machine guns. They were dressed in black and they had earpieces for communication. (Talk about top secret stuff.)

"Stop here," Yassen ordered.

The limo stopped, and Yassen stepped out of the vehicle. He bent down to act like he was tying his shoe. But then some gates opened, and he stepped back in the limo. "Okay, go, slow."

"Oh, so now you want me to go slow," the driver mouthed.

"What was that?" Yassen slid to the front of his seat, holding a gun to the driver's head. "Just do as I say."

The man nervously nodded his head and drove slowly up a ramp. Soon we came to the main house. It was huge. When I first came to Mandel's house, I thought that it was big, but this was unbelievable.

Yassen stepped out of the limo and ordered two men to come to him. "Take the girl to the room, and then kill the driver," I heard Yassen say.

I gasped. The two men grabbed my arms and took me to the room they were talking about. I knew better than to give them hard time so I let them do to me as they wished. The one man was old, about in his forties. On the other hand, the other was young, about eighteen, about a year older than me. He didn't take his eyes off me. (Let's put it this way, he was a creeper.)

They took me to the room. When they opened the door, I closed my eyes, almost afraid to see what was so special about his room. And after what I saw on my way here, if Yassen says to take me to this specific room, something has to be in it.

They walked in. "Miss," the older man said.

I opened my eyes. I looked around. Curtains, bed, bathroom, TV, dresser, desk. Just like any other room. "You are to stay here."

I looked at them and didn't say anything. "Yassen will be up shortly so don't do anything," the young one said.

They left me then, in that room. All by myself. I wrapped my arms around myself. It was cold in here. I walked over to the bed and sat on it.

The two men walked back down stair. "She's hot, too bad she's going to die," the young said.

"Don't get too attached, James," the other one said.

"I won't, Higgins," James reassured him.

"Now what do we do?"

"Yassen said to get rid of the driver," James told him.

Higgins nodded and they walked outside.

The driver stood there outside of the limo, terrified. "Sir, will you come with us, please," James asked nicely.

The driver looked at them, and then hesitantly, he nodded.

They took him over to the garden. "We thought that you would like to help us do the garden. Since you're a driver and gardener for Mandel."

The driver made a soft smile. "Oh, of course," he answered. Then he got down on his knees and started to pull weeds.

Higgins looked over at James. James nodded and looked away. Higgins pulled out his gun aimed then looked away. He pulled the trigger and the driver was no longer a driver.

They both then saw Yassen coming up the path. He was smiling. "Very good. Now keep a close watch. Mandel could be on his way. I'm going to go deal with Natalie."

They nodded and left to do what they were told. Yassen looked around him. Nothing seemed to be going wrong. Now all he needed was Mandel to make his little game start.

I stayed sitting on the bed. I didn't know what to do. It felt like I was kidnapped by a person who I thought was my friend. But then I thought about it. He was my friend.

I got up and walked over to the window and looked out. I still couldn't get over at how big this place was. I looked over to the front of the house. I saw the limo. But then I saw James and Higgins. They walked past the limo. Looking closer, I noticed that Higgins was holding something. I squinted my eyes. I saw the shape of the object. Then I saw the face. Higgins was caring the driver over his shoulder.

I gasped and stepped back. I turned around and screamed. In front of me stood Yassen with his hands crossed in front of him. He smiled. "I'm sorry, Natalie. Did I scare you?" he asked me.

Looking at him, I took in a deep breath. "No, you did not."

He smiled again and walked past me to the window. Without turning myself, I turned my head. He was over at the window looking out. He spotted Higgins walking down a path with the driver on his back. "Oh, don't worry about him. He wasn't important like you," he assured me.

I rolled my eyes. "Thank you. That makes me feel special. I'm important so I won't be killed."

He put up his pointer finger and turned to look at me. "I never said that you won't be killed. I just said that what happened to that man won't happen to you. I won't have Higgins carry you over his shoulder."

I stared at him. "What happened to you? I thought you were nice."

He laughed. "Well, I guess you thought wrong—"

He was interrupted by gunshots. At the same time, we rushed over to the window. About thirty of his men were in front of the house, shooting at a limo coming in. Then six more cars came behind it. The rushed out Mandel and Alistair. *They're here to rescue me*, I thought.

Yassen looked at me. He grabbed my arm and pulled me away from the window. "You will do exactly as I say. Or you will end up like that man," he said as he dragged me out of the room.

He pulled me down the stairs. We went to the back of the house. We went out of the door to the terrace, but there were guys shooting too. I recognized one of Mandel's men and yelled. Yassen put his hand over of my mouth and pulled out his gun.

We dashed to the left. He threw me onto the ground. I fell on my shoulder. I heard it pop. (It's funny how ever since I started to live with Mandel, I got hurt enough to last a lifetime.)

I started to get up, but people kept firing at me. I looked over at Yassen. He looked like a person you would find in the movies. He had black on and was like dodging bullets. In another circumstance, I would call him a hero. But right now, he was everything but that.

I looked over the wall that I was behind. There were like twelve people firing at Yassen. And all of those people were on my side. Then I looked behind me. Twenty people came out of the doorway with guns. (And they weren't here to make peace.) They started helping Yassen. They were shooting my people.

I ducked down then. My shoulder hurt. I looked over again. A man fell down. He wasn't dead either. He was still alive. I thought about how painful it would be to get shot like that.

My focus then turned back on Yassen. He got shot! But not severely. Well, when you get shot, it's always severe. But he only got shot in the arm. And Mafia people are really tough from what I saw so it wasn't very severe.

Yassen quickly put his hand to his shoulder. He pulled it away, and his hand turned red. He took a deep breath then continued shooting. Then I heard my name. "Natalie!"

I turned toward my name. Alistair! He was over on the far side of the wall. He was with three other guys who looked to be around his age. I quickly jumped up to my feet. I looked over at the guys who were on my side. Only about four were left. All the others were either dead or wounded. It's like they just dropped dead. (Not a pretty sight. I mean, really, when you watch movies about the Mafia and it shows, like, about how bad it is, this is the real thing. It's like on John Wayne. A classic gun-down.)

I looked away from them and turned back to Alistair. He motioned for me to come toward him. I nodded and started to run toward him. Then Alistair pointed his gun in my direction. My face turned terrified. What was going on? His eyes turned furious. Then he pulled the trigger. I ducked. Then got up. I looked at him. He was smiling at me again.

I turned around for a second. I saw Yassen on his knees. Oh, that was he was pointing at. I ran to him. He started to run to me too. His friends were smiling. He reached me first. He picked me up and hugged me. I never thought that I would be this happy to see him.

He put me down and I put my hand up to say hi to his friends. Then I remembered that my shoulder popped out and grabbed it with my other hand as a natural reaction. Alistair looked at me. "You okay?"

I nodded. "Yeah, it's only my shoulder. Where's Mandel?" I asked.

Alistair pointed to the front of the house. "He holding down up there. This is almost over."

I looked at him. I really felt like I was in a war or something. It was strange. We started to walk fast then run to the front of the house. When we got there, Mandel was walking into the house with five other guys behind, holding their guns in front of them.

Then Alistair handed me something. He put it in my hands. "It's your gun. I found it inside when I came looking for you. Stay here, I'm going to take the path to look around."

I nodded. I was kind of scared. Being here all by myself. I walked over and leaned up against the limo. Then I heard something behind then a tree. I stood up and pointed my gun. "Hello," I said.

No one answered, and out came a person (obviously). My mouth dropped. It was James. I pointed my gun at him. "Don't come any closer," I told him. "I'll shoot."

He didn't stop but kept walking toward me. "Don't shoot. I'm on your side. Besides, I'm unarmed. And you wouldn't shoot an unarmed man, would you?" he asked.

I looked at him but didn't change position. "How do I know you're telling the truth and you're not just trying to trick me into putting my gun down?"

He shook his head. "No, I'm not. If you don't believe me, then ask Alistair. He'll tell you."

"He's not here right now."

He nodded. "Well, that's obvious. Well I'm just going to go into the house and look for Mandel. You know, since I'm on your side."

I put my gun down. What could I do? He was unarmed. I watched as he went into the house. Then I walked over and leaned on the limo once again. Soon, I saw Alistair come down the path and walk toward me. I smiled and waved with my good shoulder.

He walked slowly. I don't really know why. I guess because he didn't have a reason to hurry. I looked past him. It was the path to the terrace. That's where I last saw Yassen. And he was now dead.

I looked back at Alistair. That's when I noticed that he was limping. I looked for blood but didn't see any. He smiled at me again. And well, I smiled back. But then my smiled turned to terror. Coming down the path was Yassen. He stopped in the middle of the path. He pulled up his gun and pointed it at Alistair.

Without thinking, I pulled up my gun. I quickly aimed and fired. I didn't know if I shoot him or if I completely missed and accidently shot Alistair. Because of the backfire and my bad shoulder, I fell back.

As soon as I could, I got up. By then, the three friends of Alistair were over by Yassen. Alistair was still pointing his gun around, checking for anyone else who might want to take a shot. Then he went over to his buddies. "Who made that shoot this far away?" asked one of the guys.

I ran up to them. I looked down at the body. I did that. I looked away. "She did," the other dude said.

Alistair looked at me. "I need to give you more credit next time," he said.

I made a sarcastic smile and said, "Oh, thanks. Is this war . . . fight thing done? Because I think I had enough of it for a while."

Alistair smiled at me as Mandel and James ran out of the house toward us. "What happened?" he asked. "Everything okay?"

Alistair smiled. "Yep."

Mandel looked down at Yassen eyes. Then he looked over at me. "Sorry," I said innocently. "He was going after Alistair."

The other guys, meaning, the three dudes who I found out were Caleb, John, and Max laughed. James made a little chuckle too. "Well, son, there you go. If you ever need a woman to shoot a gun, just put yourself in danger, and she'll do a good job" Mandel said to Alistair.

I didn't get what was so funny. I didn't know if it was because I was a girl or just because what he said just didn't make sense. "Yeah, well can we go home now," I asked.

Mandel nodded. "Yeah, let's go."

CHAPTER 29

The drive home from M2's house was quiet. Even though it was supposed to be happy. Why wasn't it happy? I'm back, we got Yassen. (I'll always remember him as he was before. Nice.)

I looked over a Mandel. He smiled at me. "Good to have ya home," he told me.

I smiled. "Yep," I said.

We didn't really say anything else until we got home. When I got out of the car, Alistair walked up to me. "You okay?" he asked me.

I looked at him. "Yeah, why wouldn't I be?"

"You killed a man today. Aren't you a little upset?"

Then I remembered what I did. Yassen was going to kill Alistair. What was I supposed to do? Just stand there hoping he would miss from ten feet away?

"Oh, yeah. I almost forgot," I said, suddenly sounding depressed.

"Well, I want you to know that it's okay."

I turned to him. "I know. But still, I just ended someone's life."

Then I turned and walked inside without him.

Over the next couple of weeks, things have been getting back to normal. I have been taking Shadow on walks. Prinella and I have even been talking more. We would take walks through the paths and talk like normal friends.

Alistair and I have been spending more time with each other. And then for Prinella's birthday. We held a big party for her.

Then one day I was up in my room thinking about all that has happened to me. I've been living with Mandel for almost two years.

Being seventeen now, I look at things differently. And now, looking back, I realized how lucky I was to live with them.

Then Alistair came in the door. "You wanna go on a ride?" he asked me.

"You mean on a horse?" I asked him back.

"No, on a train. Of course, a horse."

I looked out the window. "Okay."

We decided to make it a race. As soon as we were on our horses. We went out into the field. Like before back in Tahiti, I got the advantage because I started before him.

I could feel the breath swish past my face. I would close my eyes every couple of minutes. Soon I saw a figure past me. It was Alistair. He raced out in front of me. I tried to go faster, but it didn't work. I was going to lose.

Alistair stopped when he crossed the line that we marked as the finish line. I stopped then too. I got down off my horse and looked at him. "Ha-ha," he said to me.

I shook my head. "It's only one win," I told him, trying to not act mad.

He made a face at me to show that he was sorry. "Oh, baby girl. Are you mad now?" he said like a baby.

"Shut up," I told him. I crossed my arms and turned my back to him.

Then he came up. He grabbed my one arm and put it over his shoulder. Then he picked me up. I wrapped my other hand onto his other shoulder, scared I might fall.

"I'm not going to drop ya," he told me, almost offended.

"I know," I said, a smile starting to take shape on my face.

"What are you doing?" I asked him.

"We're going to take a walk," he said as he carried down small hill.

I know it might not sound true, but he did carry for the next twenty minutes. Then he put me down because I wanted to pick flowers.

I looked around. The country surrounded us. I smiled. "What is it?" Alistair asked.

I shrugged. I looked at the sun as it started to fade down over a mountain far away. "Nothing, I just can't believe I'm here."

I couldn't believe I was there. Life seems so surprising. Who knows the next day I could, well, never mind, I don't know what the next day could bring.

Until the sun went down, Alistair and I just stayed out there. Looking around, exploring. I was happy.

CHAPTER 30

I got up from my book; I was finally finished. It took me about two years to write it. I was still shocked that I remembered everything since I was fourteen. I've been writing it ever since I started to live with Mandel when I was sixteen. But now I'm seventeen and a half.

You might be confused about what s going on here. I'll explain it to you. What you just read was the past since I was fourteen. When I first came to live with Mandel, I thought that I would write a book about what has been going on. And what you just read was the book that I've been writing. I hope it makes sense. However, from here on out, is what has been happening in the present.

The door opened, and in walked Alistair. "Hey, how is it going?" Alistair asked me.

"I'm finished," I responded.

"Really? How long is it?"

"Well, I don't know, I didn't count."

"Um, cool."

He took the book from me and skimmed through it. "This is cool. Well that is if I'm in it. Am I in it? I better be."

I laughed. "Of course. Everyone is."

"I can't wait to read it."

I smiled at him when a knock came from the door. The door opened, and Mandel came in. I smiled at him. "Hey, what's going on?" he asked.

"Natalie just finished her book," Alistair answered. "And I'm in it."

Mandel walked over. "May I see it?"

He skimmed through it just as Alistair did. "May I read some?" Mandel asked.

I thought about it for a while. "Why not?" I replied.

The door was open; we were on a major highway. I was in the back of the van with my hands tied.

I was drowsy from the night before, but I managed to stay awake. Lar Mandal #2 was up front, talking to two other guys.

Soon, one of them came over to me and pulled me up. He was big and ugly and had a bad odor, but that's not the point.

They were talking in a different language so I couldn't understand them. (My guess was that it was Latin.) The big ugly guy stared to push me. He then untied me and shoved me over to Mandal #2.

All three stared at me. Mandal #2 soon grabbed my arm. He gave me an evil smile. I didn't know what it meant.

His tight grip numbed my arm. He dragged me over to the opened door to the van. His strong, muscular arm tilted my head in an angle so I could get a good look at the pack of cars in the back of us.

Alistair looked at me. "It seems so real." Alistair and I started to crack up laughing.

Mandel looked at both of us with a questioning expression on his face. "Do I want to know?"

"No, it's a joke between us," I said.

Mandel started to laugh. "What's so funny?" Alistair asked.

"It's a joke between us," Mandal said, mimicking us. "How cute."

Before he could say anything else, Alistair was chasing him across and around the room.

I knew I shouldn't, but I couldn't help it, I was laughing like crazy. I have been living here in Malta for about three years, and I really have gotten to love it and Mandel and Alistair and everyone else whom I have gotten to know. I don't know what's going to happen in the future, but I hope that someday, I will be able to call Mandel my father.

"Guys, guys, okay, that's enough. Get out, I need to get ready. I'm going into town," I yelled playfully.

They stopped as I commanded them. "Oh, can I come with you?" Alistair asked.

"Sure. I'll be leaving in an hour."

I got ready in about a half hour, with thirty minutes to spare. I went outside and to the back of the house. Making sure nobody was watching, I carefully picked a few flowers from the garden and walked out to the big oak tree to where Carlos's grave was.

For the last few months (eight months), I have been putting fresh roses on his grave for I remember those were the ones that he always got me for my birthday. I knelt down to lower myself to his level. Without crying, I placed the flowers on the bed of dirt that lay over my best friend. It was for me that he lay there still and alone.

Alistair soon joined me. He knelt down as I was and put his hand on my shoulder. It was a comfort that I longed for the longest time. "Come, let us go into town and have fun," Alistair said as he stood up. He held out his hand to help me up. Grateful, I took it.

CHAPTER 31

Alistair and I came back from town, happy and unaware of the news that was going to be put upon us in a few minutes. We walked in the house to where Mandel was waiting for us.

"Father, I thought you would be in bed. It is 11:00 p.m.," Alistair informed his father.

"I needed to stay up to tell you the news that is good yet bad. We are scheduled to leave for Italy tomorrow," Mandel said. "I am sorry. Good night."

As he walked up the stairs, I turned to be sure no one would see my emotions. Alistair put his hands on my shoulders and turned me toward him. "How could he do this?" I begged.

"It is not his fault," Alistair defended. "You knew that we would have to go sometime."

"It is not the leaving I am upset about. It's that we have to leave . . ." I couldn't finish, but I think Alistair knew what I was going to say because he pulled me closer to comfort me. However, I pulled away and ran to my room.

When I got there, I was shocked to see all of my things packed in boxes. Everything but clothing for tomorrow morning. Without even getting into my PJs, I went to bed. My pillow soaked with my tears. For the rest of the night, I didn't get much sleep.

I wasn't mad about leaving, only leaving without Carlos. While he was dying in my arms, I promised that I would never leave him. I know that it sounds awkward and silly, but that's what I promised him. Now I won't be able to follow through with it. (I always got mad when I couldn't keep my promises.)

I woke up multiple times in the night. As I said before, I didn't sleep much. I somewhat felt like I failed. About two years ago, my parents were killed because M2 got jealous. Then I was his next target. Meanwhile, Mandel was taking me in and showing me what my parents went through. Only I had it much easier. Mandel is now like a father to me, and his son is my boyfriend. (So much happened.) In addition, I lost my best friend.

I woke up in the morning's light. I didn't want to get up. I knew what awaited me. I was going to have to leave. I covered my head in my pillow, still damp from the terrible night that I just had.

I looked around, everything was gone; they must have came in earlier and got it.

Soon there was a knock at the door followed by, "Time to get up."

Slowly, I eased myself out of my bed that I slept in for so long. I got dressed and regretfully made my way down stairs. When I got there, I saw Mandel pacing back and forth and Alistair following his steps.

As soon as Mandel saw me, he motioned for me to come faster. "Come now, we are already late for our flight," he said.

Without smiling, I nodded and followed them out the door. Before I got in the limo, I looked up at Mandel. "May I please go and say good-bye?" I pleaded.

He nodded, and I ran off. I picked some more flowers and put them down next to the ones I laid yesterday.

I started to cry as I knelt down. "Carlos, I am so sorry. I am sorry that you died and for everything else that I did. I didn't mean it. I feel that I failed to keep my promise to you. If I could stay here, I would," I said without any caution as to who was listening.

I put my hands to my face to cover my tears. I felt a hand on my shoulder. I expected to see Alistair standing looking down at me, but I was surprised I saw Mandel.

He knelt down next to me and said, "I know how you feel. He was my son. You don't know the pain that I am feeling and the shame that I feel having to leave my son . . . my son behind. I watched him grow, comforted him when he fell, and punished him when he failed to do good. And now I won't get to see nothing."

He put his hand to his mouth and gave a little gasp of what I thought was a comfort to him. "Everyone says that if you're part of the Mafia, you're cold, heartless, and tough. I might be tough, but I am warm and I have a heart for those who need it."

I didn't know what to say. After two years of knowing him and seeing him every day, this was the first time I ever saw him cry.

He looked over at me, "He saved your life and didn't think nothing of his. You should feel proud more than sorry. He thought a lot about you, Natalie. He would write letters to me when he was living with my wife's sister, saying about all the fun you have together."

He left it at that and helped me up. "Hopefully we can come back sometime," I said.

He nodded. "I hope so too."

We got in the limo and started driving away. When we passed the gates, I watched them close and whispered to myself, "Good-bye, my friend."

Four Years Later

The last four years have been nothing but moving here and moving there. I am now twenty-one and engaged to Alistair. Four months till our wedding, and for my early wedding present, Alistair brought me back to Malta.

As we drove in the driveway, I watched the gates open and close. It brought back so many memories.

When I got out of the limo, I walked swiftly into the house. The smell brought tears to my eyes. I raced through the house. I went to every single room. However, when I came a room that said, "Carlos's, keep out," I looked down and headed out.

As I came out the back, I saw the big oak tree. It was full of bushes and grass. I went over, got on my hands and knees, and started to pull them out. When I was done, I went and got the fresh roses that I bought at a supermarket.

I laid down the roses and said, "How are you doing? Okay? The last couple of years have been hectic. Nevertheless, I promise to see you every year from now on. However, there has not been a day that went by that I have not thought about you. Well, I better go, Alistair is waiting for me. We're getting married by the way. Anyway, I love ya. See you soon."

As I got up and started to walk away, I heard a noise and turned around. There two white doves in the air. I smiled and walked away. I knew that he could hear me. Either in the ground or in heaven. Wherever he was, I'll never forget him.

I walked out to the limo. "All done?" Alistair asked me.

"Yep, thanks."

I got into the limo and started to drive off. Before my parents died, I never knew what family was like. I loved them. In a distant kind of way. When they died, it bothered me that I did not feel worse than I did. Now, I know how it feels to lose someone who really meant a lot to you.

I head now into the world. I don't know what's going to happen next. Who knows, I could *drop dead* in the next minute. Things happen that are the unexpected. (Especially in the Mafia.)

As we drove away, I looked back. Just like four years ago, I was leaving my friend. However, this time, he will always be in my heart.

Edwards Brothers, Inc.
Thorofare, NJ USA
July 7, 2011